Praise for

Jan Moran's *Love, California Series*

Empowering romance with a touch of suspense

"An engrossing view into the world of beautiful people with an ending that will leave you wanting more."
— *New York Times* & *USA Today* bestselling author Melissa Foster

"Jan Moran is the new queen of the epic romance."
— *USA Today* Bestselling Author Rebecca Forster, Author of *Expert Witness*

"Jan Moran's heroines are strong women…this series is fast-paced and well written."
— Karen Laird, Under the Shade Tree Reviews

"The characters reach out of the pages and pull you into their lives, and they stay with you long after you close the book."
— Hannah Fielding, Author of *The Echoes of Love*

Praise for *The Winemakers* (St. Martin's Griffin)

"Readers will devour this page-turner as the mystery and passions spin out. VERDICT: A solid pick for fans of historical romances combined with a heartbreaking mystery."
– *The Library Journal*

"As she did with fragrance and scent-making in *Scent of Triumph*, Moran weaves knowledge of wine and winemaking into this intense family drama."– *Booklist*

"Absolutely adored *The Winemakers*. Beautifully layered and utterly compelling. Intriguing from start to finish. A story not to be missed."
— Jane Porter, USA Today & New York Times Bestselling Author of *It's You* and *The Good Woman*

"We were spellbound by the thread of deception weaving the book's characters into a tangled web, and turned each page anticipating the outcome."
– *The Mercury News*

Praise for *Scent of Triumph* (St. Martin's Griffin)

"A well-spun and sweeping novel about a fearless, headstrong woman. Spanning multiple continents and set against the backdrop of World War II, Jan Moran deftly weaves plotlines and tackles tough issues, all to a satisfying conclusion. Add in glimpses of the high-end fragrance trade, and *Scent of Triumph* offers a thoroughly engaging tale, rich in all five senses."
— Michelle Gable, Author of *A Paris Apartment*

"A heartbreaking, evocative read that will transport readers to another place and time and not let go. I could not turn the pages fast enough!"
— Anita Hughes, Author of *Lake Como*

"*Scent of Triumph* has a dedicated look into the history of the world of fashion; recommended."— Midwest Book Review

"A gripping World War II story of poignant love and devastating, heart-wrenching loss. The perfumes are so beautifully described, you can smell them wafting up from the pages."
— Gill Paul, Author of *The Affair*

"The tragedies of war, conflicts in family, love, and passion for perfumery paint a realistic, historical portrait of some of the fragrance industry's most famous women who created today's top cosmetic firms."
— Marvel Fields, Chairman, American Society of Perfumers

"From war-torn Europe to the sunny climes of Southern California, *Scent of Triumph* is a captivating tale of love, loss, determination and reinvention."
— Karen Marin, Givenchy Paris

Style

A Love, California Novel
Book Number 5

by
Jan Moran

SUNNY PALMS
PRESS

Library of Congress Cataloging-in-Publication Data
Moran, Jan.
/ by Jan Moran

ISBN 978-1-942073-90-1 (softcover)
ISBN 978-1-942073-88-8 (ebooks)

Printed in the U.S.A.
Cover design by Silver Starlight Designs
Cover images copyright 123RF

For Inquiries Contact:
Sunny Palms Press
9663 Santa Monica Blvd STE 1158
Beverly Hills, CA, USA
www.SunnyPalmsPress.com
www.JanMoran.com

For Zoë, who was born with style.

Books by Jan Moran

Contemporary

The Love, California Series:

Flawless

Beauty Mark

Runway

Essence

Style

Sparkle

20th Century Historical

The Winemakers: A Novel of Wine and Secrets

Scent of Triumph: A Novel of Perfume and Passion

*Life is a Cabernet: A Companion Wine Novella to
The Winemakers*

NonFiction

Vintage Perfumes

To hear about Jan's new books first and get special offers, join Jan's VIP Readers Club at www.JanMoran.com and get a free ebook.

1

New York City

"THIS WAY, PENELOPE, to your right."

Penelope stepped from the limousine and paused on the red carpet. With natural, fluid motions, she swirled her translucent violet cape and tossed her lavender-streaked tresses to strike a nonchalant pose that was second nature to her. Mentally calculating light sources and intensity—and how those combined with the angles and planes of her face—she glanced in the photographer's direction long enough for the woman's digital camera to whir through frames in split seconds.

She pouted, then relaxed into a smile, to give the editor a choice. Make the photographer's job easy; that was her theory, and she credited this approach to her success.

Another voice rang out, raspy and gruff. "Hey Penny, who are you wearing?"

"Fianna Fitzgerald." Penelope turned toward a grungy photographer and repeated her process.

His camera snapped intermittently as he tried to focus shots for whatever publication he was shooting for—though many paparazzi were independent, selling celebrity shots to the highest bidder. In her years of modeling, Penelope knew a lot of them, at least by sight, but she'd never seen this bungling, lanky man in faded black clothes. Still, New York's Fashion Week drew a wide variety of crowds. She remained patient, feeling sorry for this obvious newcomer. The man fumbled with his camera; he'd never be Richard Avedon, but then, few fashion photographers were such legends.

"Fitzgerald. Name is kind of familiar," he said, fidgeting with his camera while other photographers stepped beside him and took his shot. "Is she someone?"

Besides his naiveté, Penelope sensed something unsettling about him, but she continued. "She's a new fashion designer from Ireland, living in America." She'd met Fianna a few years ago through Fianna's aunt, Davina, a supermodel who had encouraged her to enter modeling as a profession. Now, Fianna was one of her closest friends.

"Oh yeah, the Fitzgerald Flop." He smirked. "She sure played that one to the hilt."

What a jerk. Strolling beside the bank of media lining the entry, Penelope spied photographers from *Vogue* and *The New York Times*. She angled a hand on her hip and stretched her leg through a slit in her flowing skirt, though she didn't let her expression reveal that the gruff man's comments annoyed her.

Her friend's debut runway show in Dublin had been sabotaged, and a model had been seriously injured. The media splashed the incident across the tabloid pages, and Fianna nearly lost everything she'd worked so hard for. If not for a stroke of brilliance in embracing the moniker and creating an edgy street line around it, her friend would have been bankrupt. Penelope and other friends had pitched in to help Fianna salvage her career and see her dreams come to fruition.

"Hey, Penny—"

"Sorry, have to run." She was giving a speech and didn't want to be late, but there was also something about that man that was disturbing. Penelope swirled around, her iridescent train rippling in her wake. Dangling amethyst earrings brushed her long neck as she ascended the steps.

From the corner of her eye, she saw the grungy photographer turn to leave, though a bevy of other models and celebrities strode behind her. That struck her as odd; there were still many good shots to be had. She had developed a talent for looking beneath the glossy veneer.

Once inside, Penelope paused to take in the glittering scene. Dance music thumped, ruby and indigo lights sparkled, and a mélange of perfume wafted above it all.

"Penelope, over here." A tall women with wild red hair waved to her. She wondered if the photographers had stopped Fianna on her way in.

As Penelope cut through the celebrity-studded fashion crowd, *Fashion News Daily* editor Aimee Winterhaus said hello, Tom Ford kissed her cheek, and André Leon Talley, a legendary contributing editor to *Vogue*, caught her eye and gestured his approval of her ensemble.

Just past André, a highly competitive new model slid a narrowed look her way, and next to her was Monica Graber, a model she'd known for years who'd betrayed her. Her ex-best friend. Monica usually adopted a haughty air around her, but today Monica's eyes darted away and her leg shook, nervous tics Penelope recognized.

Penelope swiveled with studied nonchalance, avoiding the distasteful pair. As a fresh young model from Copenhagen, she'd matured in this mercurial world of friends and frenemies, where fashion was cutthroat business and burned through weak models like dry twigs.

"You were magnificent today," Fianna said, flinging her arms open in greeting.

Earlier in the day, Penelope had walked for a top designer at Skylight at Moynihan Station on 33rd Street in a historic post office venue. The beautiful Beaux-Arts exterior opened to an enormous, light-filled postal sorting room that was a perfect venue for fashion shows.

As Penelope hugged Fianna, she could feel her friend quivering with enthusiasm. The last thing she wanted was to dampen her friend's mood with a remark about the dreadful photographer out front. Judging from Fianna's mood, she probably hadn't seen him. "So what do you think of this madness?"

Fianna was so excited, her freckled face seemed lit from within. "Davina used to let me tag along when I was a kid, but Fashion Week is much crazier now. What an incredible experience this is. So many stars from Hollywood are here, too."

Penelope laughed. "Come on, you must be used to that in

14

L.A. by now. Don't celebs shop at your boutique?"

"New York has a different vibe. It's the Big Apple. The concrete jungle." Fianna started humming the Alicia Keys song about New York.

"I'm glad you got to come." Penelope added with a wink, "There's a good chance your design I'm wearing might be published in *Vogue* magazine. Wouldn't be surprised if you get business off it."

When Penelope told her that André Leon Talley had shown his approval, Fianna's mismatched eyes widened with delight. Fashion Week was the longstanding event where everyone in fashion met for business.

"Hope you're right. I'd love to pay off my student loans for FIDM."

Penelope glanced over her shoulder. "Some of the instructors from the New York branch of the Fashion Institute for Design and Merchandising are usually here. I'll let you know if I see them." Penelope admired the way Fianna had handled the early trials in her fledging career with unflagging determination and creativity.

"Where's Davina?" Penelope asked, looking around. "I haven't much time before I have to give my speech."

"Behind us," Fianna said, turning to a crowd gathered behind them.

An elegant woman in a liquid silver sheath emerged from the group. She wore a sapphire-and-hammered-silver collar encircling her long neck. Her azure eyes shimmered, and her thick platinum mane flowed around her shoulders.

"Right here, darling," Davina said, her voice laced with an Irish lilt. She touched her gleaming collar. "I'm talking with Elena and her friends about this stunning piece she designed for me."

Originally from Australia, Elena Eaton designed fine jewelry and had a shop next to Fianna's studio on Robertson Boulevard in Los Angeles. An athletic brunette clad in a sleek, ebony gown that showcased her exquisite jewelry, Elena waved at her and called out, "How're you doing?"

Penelope smiled and waved back. She knew several of the young stars were wearing Elena's pieces today, and she couldn't be happier for her friend. She'd recommended her jewelry to several designers who'd chosen bold pieces to accent their designs. Designers often had their own lines, or didn't accessorize at all, so this was quite a coup for a young jewelry designer.

Davina stepped back to admire Penelope's ensemble. "*Hej smukke,*" she said, her eyes twinkling.

"Well, hello beautiful yourself," Penelope said, kissing Davina on each cheek. "Are you learning Danish?"

Davina laughed. "I learned some phrases from a Danish prince at a dinner party in London a few weeks ago. You really are stunning tonight. Ready to give your talk?"

"I am."

"Garbo speaks," Davina said, sweeping her hand to mimic a headline. "I was at a silent film festival last night. You're too young to remember those days."

"So are you. Are you doing any work in New York?"

"Print gigs only. Not as crazy as catwalk life." Davina gestured across the crowded room. "Everything about this business is so different now."

"Has it really changed that much?" Penelope loved hearing about when Davina was at the pinnacle of her success. Even at the age of fifty, Davina was still a stunning woman, proving that beauty needn't diminish with age. Her famous cheekbones were still well-defined, but more than that, it was Davina's empathy, laughter, and professionalism that endeared her to so many in the industry. Penelope counted herself lucky to have had Davina as a mentor.

"Models are thinner than ever before, and there are many more temptations." Davina indicated a rail-thin model with sharp cheekbones and sunken cheeks who languished near a bar. "Or maybe I see it more clearly now from a distance."

"That's exactly my point tonight." A petite woman with horn-rimmed glasses caught Penelope's eye. "Excuse me, I think it's show time."

The woman clasped a clipboard to her chest. "Miss Plessen, we'd like to begin. Come with me now."

Davina winked at her. *Held og lykke.*

"It's not luck I need," Penelope replied. "It's everyone's support."

Penelope accompanied the woman to the stage, as Fianna, Davina, and Elena followed.

The area in front of the raised stage area was crowded. "Pardon me," Penelope said, brushing past a well-built man in a tuxedo. He wore mirrored glasses and had longish chestnut hair.

Very L.A. Something about him seemed familiar, though she pushed the thought aside. She had to gather her thoughts for her presentation.

The lights went up, and the designer she'd walked for earlier today, Ruben Lars Eriksen, a fellow Dane who also lived in Los Angeles, stepped under the floodlights to introduce her.

"Penelope Plessen is a chameleon," Ruben began. "She's the model so many of us turn to when we're creating a new look because of her unique ability to morph into what we've imagined in our mind. She translates our vision, bringing it to life on the stage and page. Last year, she also brought her vision and style to cosmetics with the launch of Penelope of Denmark for High Gloss Cosmetics."

Penelope nodded toward Olga Kaminsky, the CEO of High Gloss, with whom she had worked in Los Angeles on the makeup line. Due to fierce competition and an industry preference for youth, runway models often had short careers, so Penelope was anxious to create a business that could live on beyond her modeling career.

Ruben held out a hand to Penelope. "Besides beauty and fashion, Penelope has an important initiative for our industry that she'd like to share with you tonight."

Amid applause, Penelope took the stage and thanked Ruben. She stepped to the podium and adjusted the microphone. Gazing over the crowd, she noticed the unkempt photographer from the red carpet. She thought he'd left, yet there he was, lurking on the edge of the crowd, smirking. She found his presence unsettling, so she turned away, drew a breath, and began.

18

"During the past fifty years, the silhouette of our industry has evolved to the point where many of our finest young models are suffering—and even dying—of eating disorders and drugs." Penelope paused to compose herself, thinking about the friends she'd lost, but most of all, recalling her mother's private struggle with depression and anorexia.

"These issues aren't only about us. They also affect those in our communities who want to look like models and emulate this behavior. It's time we take action for our health, and for our industry as models of behavior. With France, Italy, Israel, and other countries enacting laws to ban the use of malnourished models, I'm happy to announce a new healthy assistance and rehab program with facilities in California and soon, in Europe and other regions, too. This is made possible by leaders and donors in our industry. It's important we open the conversation and—"

"Hey Penny." From the edge of the crowd, a man's menacing voice rang out.

Few people called her Penny. Recognizing the odd, raspy voice, she turned toward it, just as the photographer she'd met outside stretched his arm toward her. Something flashed in his hand—

A man nearby chopped his arm and lunged for the photographer while he struggled to regain his stance. People in the crowd ducked, pressed back, and scattered. Screams split the air, and cameras flashed.

Watching in horror, Penelope grabbed the microphone and ducked. "Everybody down! He's got a gun!"

While others were diving for cover, the man she'd brushed

past by the stage leapt up and scooped Penelope up in his arms. "Hey, let go of me!" Reacting, she instantly shoved her palm up against his nose.

The guy dodged her strike, taking the blow to his cheekbone instead. "Getting you to safety," he said through gritted teeth.

As the scuffle below continued, a shot rang out, and the podium splintered. All at once, the lights went off.

Adrenaline flashed through her as the man carried her away from the chaos. Penelope clasped his neck and drew up her legs, feeling his veins pumping against her skin and his heart throbbing against her chest. Was she safe with this man? She couldn't be sure, but if he'd wanted her dead he would've left her on stage.

Where were her friends? "Davina! Elena, Fianna!" All she could do was pray they were out of harm's way. Jostled against the man's chest, she tightened her grip.

Once they'd cleared the stage, he kicked open a backstage door. Finding an empty dressing room, he put her down.

Out of breath, she cried out, "I've got friends out there. We have to get to them." Davina, Elena, Fianna… and so many others.

Without acknowledging her comment, he flipped out a pen-sized flashlight, tapped it on, and handed it to her. "Use this."

Footsteps clattered in the dim hallway. "Is she okay? Let us in," cried Fianna. "We followed your screams." Davina and Elena were behind her, holding their phones with flashlight apps illuminating their way.

"They're with me." Without waiting for approval from the

man with icy mirrored glasses, Penelope grasped Fianna's trembling hands and pulled her into the room. "Is anyone hurt?"

"We're okay," Fianna said, her eyes wide with fright. "I don't think anyone was hit, but I can't be sure...."

"Lock it." The man shut the door behind him.

While Fianna and Elena clutched each other, Davina folded her into her arms. "Thank goodness you weren't hurt. That guy saved your life."

He had, hadn't he? Penelope had always prided herself on being able to care of herself, but against a bullet moving at a millisecond? She shuddered at the thought of what might have happened.

Davina kissed her cheek. "He risked his life for you. Do you know who he was?"

She had no idea, Penelope thought with a jolt. Risking his own safety, the man had acted quickly. She wished she'd gotten a better look at his face. His physique was rock solid, and she *had* felt safe in his arms, though she hated to admit her vulnerability.

His scent reminded her of... She shook her head, dispelling a disturbing memory that surged to the surface. After her heart had been broken, she found it easier not to get too attached.

"That photographer out front," Penelope began, chastising herself.

"Who?" Davina place her hands on Penelope's cheeks and searched her eyes. "Do you know who did this?"

"I'd never seen him before," Penelope said, a sickening feeling churning within her. She should've said something, alerted someone. "Oh Davina, if only I'd said something, maybe I could've stopped this from happening."

Davina pressed her to her breast, soothing her. "Darling, you couldn't have known what he was planning to do."

On the way in she'd been thinking about her speech and her friends, but maybe she could have had him questioned or removed. She swallowed hard against searing tears of guilt and regret that filled her eyes.

The sound of hysterical crying echoed in the hallway, and Penelope inched open the door to two women. "In here," she called, pulling the pair inside to safety.

Outside, screams and scuffling ensued. Davina put her arms around Fianna and Elena to calm them, and then reached out to the two panic-stricken women to bring them into the circle.

Penelope stood by the door, pressing her ear to it. No way was that lunatic getting in here.

One of the women cried out, "What will we do if the shooter tries to get in?"

"We'll stop him." Penelope set her jaw. Never before had she been singled out for violence. She had no idea why anyone would try to kill her, but there were nuts out there, and now he was a threat to everyone. Was he a fan? Had he faked his press credentials? Thoughts raced through her mind, though nothing made sense to her.

After a few minutes, the havoc outside seemed to taper off, and the lights above them flickered on.

"Thank goodness." Penelope turned off the mini-flashlight.

A knock burst at the door. "Penelope, you ladies okay in there?"

22

He knew her name. But then, she'd been introduced when she'd gone up on stage. She eased the door open to the man who'd saved her from danger.

"Shaken, that's all." For years Penelope had traveled the world to remote locations in Africa, South America, and the Middle East. She'd been trapped in political uprisings, but nothing had prepared her for a direct public attack. That is, except for the self-defense classes her parents had insisted she take when she left home to begin her career.

She peered at the muscled man who stood taller than she did—six-feet-five with her towering Manolo Blahnik heels—and stopped, agape as he stood before her, his mirrored glasses now in his hands.

"*Stefan*? What are you doing here?"

"I'm on duty."

"What the—why?" Shocked by his presence, Penelope could hardly think.

He looked past her into the room. "Everyone stay put for now."

Davina spoke up. "Has that man been caught?"

Stefan pressed a finger to his ear, and only then did Penelope realize he wore a discreet earpiece. "Not yet. He escaped in the dark. Police have surrounded the building and closed the street. They'll need to interview witnesses." He turned to face Penelope, his startling blue eyes shot with concern. "They want to talk to you."

"Of course." All at once, Penelope felt the adrenaline drain from her body, and she began to shiver. Or was it the presence of

Stefan, the man she'd thought she'd never see again? Despite her protests, he had forged into action with such authority.

But then, he always had.

"Better sit down," he said. He grabbed a bottle of water from a table and opened it for her. Pulling up a chair, he sat across from her, leaning his elbows on his knees and staring into her eyes with the direct gaze that had touched her so many years ago. "Do you know who tried to shoot you?"

Davina and the other women sat down, watching them.

Shaking her head, Penelope blinked. His eyes were clouded with concern, just as when he'd broken off their relationship in the worst way. She drank and tried to appear calm despite her hammering pulse. "He was taking photos outside, but now I doubt he was a photographer."

"Why do you say that?"

"He didn't know how to use his camera."

"And how did you know that?"

"While their cameras are pointed at *me*, I'm watching *them*."

Stefan studied her for a moment, a corner of his mouth turning up in approval. Seemingly satisfied, he tapped his earpiece and said, "Roger that." To her, he added. "The police are on their way back. Glad you're not hurt." He stood and walked to the door.

"Stefan." It took all the energy Penelope had to utter his name.

He hesitated, his hand on the knob. "Yes?"

"Will you come back?" Penelope crossed her arms. *Damn it,*

24

where did that *come from?*

His expression gave no indication of the relationship they'd once had. "If that's what you want."

The two women who'd sought refuge with them followed Stefan out the door, and as soon as the door closed, Davina clasped her trembling hands. She inclined her head toward the closed door. "That man with the Paul Newman eyes. Is that *your* Stefan?"

Penelope nodded, still trying to process what had just occurred. "He's changed. His hair… it's a little longer." But he still had the same piercing blue eyes that took her breath away. "I never thought I'd see him again."

Fianna and Elena traded a look before Fianna spoke up. "Excuse me, that incredible specimen of a man… you *know* him?"

Penelope rubbed her bare arms and blew out a breath. "I haven't seen him in a long time." Since the day she and Monica had parted ways as friends.

"Wow. You kept that hunk of man from us?" Elena pressed her lips together. "He looks like a Navy SEAL."

"Actually, he was." Penelope stared at the door. *Of all the men…*

Tossing her fiery mane over one shoulder, Fianna waggled her eyebrows. "Oh, my God, if it weren't for Niall—"

In a release of intense fear, nerves gave way to a twitter of laughter in the room.

"Hands off, you two lovebirds adore each other," Elena cut in, playfully slapping Fianna's hand. She turned to Penelope. "And you never dated him?"

Penelope felt her face flush. "I didn't say *that*."

Elena's mouth formed a silent O, while Davina shook her head in warning. The last thing Penelope wanted to discuss was her relationship with Stefan.

Fianna leaned forward, her eyes flashing. "Stefan's so hot. The way he scooped you up and looks at you, I think he's interested. What happened?"

"Too complicated to explain." Penelope met Davina's eyes, which were rimmed with concern. She'd cried in her arms when Stefan left, and ever since, she'd compared every man she met to him. With her busy career, she didn't have time for serious dating, so it had been for the best. Of that she was certain.

Davina lifted a brow and squeezed her hand. "Fianna, Elena, enough with the questions, Our Penelope's in shock."

"I'm okay." Penelope shook her head, though she wasn't sure if she was trying to convince Davina or herself.

Two police officers arrived and set to work taking their statements. Penelope told them everything she could remember, but the only thing that seemed to help them was that she didn't think he was a photographer.

"Can you think of any motive this man might've had?" asked the officer who sat before her.

Fianna cut in. "Motive? For Penelope? You've got to be kidding, that guy's a mentaller," she exclaimed. When the police office looked confused at her Irish slang, she put her hands on her hips and huffed. "How about just bat-shit crazy?"

Penelope nodded with a rueful grin. "Next question."

"Have you received any odd correspondence from anyone?

26

Anything through social media?"

"I get the regular love letters and suggestive Anthony Weiner-style photos, but I don't know if any of those could be traced to this."

"We'll need to see those."

"I trashed them." Penelope crossed her legs and tapped her foot as the officer shook his head. "What's the point of keeping that stuff?"

"Isn't it obvious now?" He shook his head and spoke to her as though she were a child. "When you chase the spotlight, you have to take precautions."

Penelope crossed her arms and glared at the officer. "I *never* chased the spotlight, that's not why I'm in this line of work. I was a skinny fourteen-year-old, five-foot-ten-inch swimmer when someone asked if I wanted to make extra money wearing new clothes one weekend. So I did."

The detective glared back. "Lot of models claw their way to the top."

"I work hard. That's how I got where I am today."

"Uh-huh." He scratched a note. "Your photos are everywhere. You sell photos or stories to the media?"

"And if I did?" She huffed. "Print campaigns for brands and magazines—that's my job. As for the media, yes, they follow me. If I can leverage that for a good cause, I do. But no, I don't sell stories or photos to the tabloids." Penelope tapped her dark purple nails on the table, wondering when Stefan would return. And why she wanted him to.

The detective dotted an *i* with a jab. "Let's try this again.

Anyone who's contacted you lately that you can recall?"

Penelope tried to take calming breaths, but found she could hardly draw in air. "I'm trying to be helpful, but you have no idea how many people reach out to me on social media. I don't see everything. I have a VA who helps answer messages while I'm working." Her throat threatened to close, and she pushed down an involuntary sense of panic. "Shouldn't you be out looking for that guy instead of questioning me?"

"VA?"

"Virtual assistant."

"I'll need that name." The detective flipped to a new page on his notepad and spun it around.

Penelope leaned over and printed the name. She wanted to be hopeful, but she had a sinking feeling. "Think you'll catch the guy?"

"We'll do our best."

The officer left his card with her, asking her to call if she thought of anything that could help in the investigation. He moved on to talk to Davina, Fianna, and Elena.

"Hey there." A deep voice reverberated behind her.

Penelope raised her eyes and found herself staring at Stefan again. "Hey."

"Looks like your friends will be busy for a while. Think they'd mind if we took a walk?"

Any other time the answer would've been no. "I'll tell them." Penelope crossed the room and knelt by Davina. "If I don't get out of here—"

"Go," Davina interjected. "No need to stay. I'm sure your

nerves are in tatters. I'll stay with Fianna and Elena." She arched an eyebrow toward Stefan. "You'll be all right with that one?"

"We're just taking a walk. I'll be safe with him," Penelope said, though she wasn't sure her heart would be.

Clutching her arm, Stefan cut through the crowd.

After the way he'd broken her heart, any other time Penelope would have slapped his hand off, but she let it stay, recognizing she might still need assistance in this highly charged situation. Police had cleared the party and were checking people and taking statements in the wide hallway outside the room. The mood in the anteroom was tense and jittery. Party-goers were live-streaming the chaotic scene on their phones to social media.

"Hey Penelope," a woman called out. "Are you okay?"

Across the crush of fashionable people, a sea of faces and camera phones swung her way. Feeling the heat of attention, she raised her hand and gave a thumbs-up sign, curving her lips into the semblance of a smile, though her nerves were still raw.

People she passed chimed in with their sentiments, and she thanked them as Stefan led her through the throng.

Only Monica turned away as soon as she saw her with Stefan. Monica's shimmering, ice blue dress clung to her nearly skeletal frame, revealing everything, even the tension between her shoulder blades. She had always been extremely thin but Penelope imagined that her BMI index was now below the line set by the participating countries. She wouldn't see Monica in France unless the woman started eating.

Besides, one couldn't live on vodka alone. Or whatever she was into now.

Stefan pressed his hand slightly on the small of her back in a familiar protective gesture, and Penelope stiffened. His touch still shot through her with the heat of molten lava. She pressed a hand over her heart, feeling pressure build in her chest.

He leaned close to her ear and said, "I know a place we can go where it's quiet."

Not a walk, but alone with Stefan. *If I have any sense at all*, she thought, *the answer is no*. She blinked while he stood gazing at her, waiting for her response.

2

PENELOPE GLANCED AROUND the anteroom, which was still teeming with beautiful people intent on making the best out of a gunman ruining their glamorous evening. If anything, Penelope thought they seemed almost happy about the media attention it brought forth. That was fame. Even bad press was still press. Some people even seemed excited, thrilled that they'd escaped the threat of death—as long as they weren't targeted.

Anxious to escape the flashing lights and rising voices, she met Stefan's eyes and said, "Let's go before I end up on another live stream." Surely leaving with the man who broke her heart couldn't be any worse than what this night had thrown at her. Under the intensity of his gaze, she thought, what was a little more danger now that she'd survived a bullet?

Sliding his hand to her bicep, Stefan held her protectively as he steered through a swarm of people, clearing the way for them. Questions about Stefan and Monica buzzed uncontrollably through her mind but she said nothing, offering brave smiles to the party-goers who clapped their hands and offered kind words as she passed. Luckily, she'd been cleared to leave while the police interviewed the guests before evacuating the building.

When they emerged from the venue into the brisk evening air, Penelope finally drew in a deep breath. Sounds of the city roared louder than her pounding heart, and she was thankful that the dark night would hide her emotions as shadows surrounded them. Living in the spotlight had trained her to stay composed and to convey the emotions photographers wanted, but the adrenaline and feeling of Stefan's strong hand on her arm made it more difficult to stay in control.

"This way," Stefan said, peering at her in his peripheral vision.

The police had blocked media from the entrance, but as she lifted her gaze, she spied a darkened form taking photographs from a window across the street. She turned away, feeling uneasy.

Her ears still rang with the shot, and she shuddered, recalling the moment. Stefan spoke quietly to a police officer on the sidewalk, and moments later, they slid into the backseat of his police car.

"Buddy of mine." Stefan craned his neck, still concerned for her safety. "We're not taking any chances with you."

They drove a few blocks, a distance Penelope could have easily walked—even in heels—but she was still shaken. They stopped in front of a small Art Deco apartment building, a lovely bronze-accented jewel from the last century. The officer escorted them inside the building. Once ensconced inside a narrow mirrored elevator, Stefan used a key to unlock the penthouse floor.

"Thanks for getting me out of there... and everything else." Penelope said, watching the floors tick by and trying to squelch her feelings for Stefan. "Sorry about your face. Had I known you were trying to help me, I'd have gone easier on you. All things considered."

He stood with his muscular arms folded across his broad chest and didn't flinch when she reached out to graze her fingers along the already forming bruise. "I always knew you could handle yourself," he said.

The elevator slid to a halt, and Penelope stepped out into an airy apartment decorated in a midcentury modern style. She looked around in surprise.

Low, black leather-clad banquettes anchored the living room. Plush white shag rugs dotted light bamboo floors, and colorful, splashy artwork lined the walls. A bike leaned against one wall, hand weights were stacked in a corner, and a high-tech computer system with several screens sat on a long Ikea-styled desk.

Stefan tossed his sunglasses onto a sleek glass entry table and then stepped into the kitchen. He grabbed two bottles of acai juice from the refrigerator. "Unless you want something stronger," he said, nodding toward a couple bottles of liquor. "Thought you could use a place to unwind. That must have been frightening."

"This is better." Penelope accepted the juice and drank, cooling her thirst and trying to check her distress. She glanced around the room. "Is this…?"

He raised an eyebrow in answer. "My place. Monica hated it. Never came here. I'm also licensed to practice law in New York, so I used this for business when I had cases. She preferred to stay in luxury hotels when she came to the city."

Questions raced through her mind, but she dared not ask. Instead, she glanced around, intrigued by what she saw. He'd elevated his style from his student days she'd known. "Really nice."

"Yeah." He grinned. "I grew up and realized I had a sense of style after all." He opened French doors to a balcony, checked outside, and held his hand out to her. "Fresh air?"

Penelope hesitated, but then took his hand. As she stepped out and lifted her face to the night sky, he shut off the lights in the room behind them, cloaking them in protective darkness.

Dimly lit windows from thousands of apartments surrounded them like stars come to earth to shroud them in anonymity. Though the days were still warm, the night breezes were now edged with autumn and New Yorkers had cracked their windows. Somewhere, a fireplace burned and a pianist practiced Chopin, stirring her memories.

"I just love New York this time of year." A lump rose in her throat. It was also one of the last places she'd seen Stefan in person, so many years ago. This is where he'd told her it had to be over between them. That duty had forced him to make a decision he hadn't wanted to make.

He glanced at her shoes. "Those can't be comfortable. Give me a foot," he said, patting a thigh. "I'll help you with that strap."

Penelope was too tired to argue. She lifted her foot, resting her stiletto on his firm thigh. He unfastened the tiny jewel-encrusted buckle on one slim ankle strap, and then repeated the process. As he worked on the miniature clasp, she bit her lip. The gentle touch of his large, sturdy hands was almost more than she could bear.

"You had no chance of escaping in these." Handling her ankles as though they were made of crystal, he removed her shoes and placed them inside the door.

"Much better." Penelope wiggled her pedicured toes, watching as Stefan shrugged out of his tuxedo jacket, untied his bowtie, and unfastened a couple of buttons. He was still as solid as she'd remembered.

She swung her gaze from him, blinking hard as she looked out over the twinkling lights of the city, her chest tightening.

"You okay?"

Penelope nodded, though heat coursed over her neck and face. She pressed her fingers at the corners of her eyes, but she couldn't stem the sudden moisture gathering in her eyes.

Stefan drew a white handkerchief from his jacket and handed it to her without a word.

Choking up, Penelope turned and sobbed into his chest. "I'm sorry," she said, her voice cracking. "It's all just catching up to me."

"It's hell when the adrenaline wears off."

Penelope ignored his remark. All she could think about was how thankful she was to be standing on the balcony in this moment. "You saved my life."

"No, the guard who whacked the shooter's arm saved your life." Awkwardly, he swept his arm around her, patting her back.

Penelope gripped his starched white shirt in her hand, scrunching up the fabric. Inhaling, she realized she'd been right—she *had* recognized his scent when he'd lifted her in his arms and rushed her to safety. He still wore the same eau de parfum she'd chosen for him years ago. The weekend of their six-month anniversary of dating, back when her world seemed full of endless love. Mingled with his natural masculine scent, the intoxicating result was just as she'd recalled, embedded in her memory.

One she'd tried to forget for so many years.

Just as she began to back away from him, he encircled her with both arms and drew her back to him. This time, it was his turn. Blinking rapidly, raw emotion seeped through his stoic expression.

"I'm glad you're safe," he said, his voice husky.

Penelope ran a hand over his light chestnut hair that grazed his collar, surprised at how silky it felt. "You *did* save me," she said again, allowing him his due. "I was up there on the stage trying to warn everyone in the crowd. If you hadn't whisked me away, that guy might've gotten off another shot at me."

This time, Stefan didn't reply. He ran a hand through her hair and buried his face against her neck. She could feel his heart pounding against hers, his breath warm against her neck. *How easy it would be....* And how painful to traverse that path with him again. No. *Never give your heart.* That had become her motto after he'd called it quits.

Drying her eyes, she murmured, "Stefan...we can't..."

Slowly, he released her and stepped away, gripping the railing on the balcony as if he were the one who needed support. She leaned against her end of the rail.

Penelope could only watch him, this magnificent man who'd held her heart for so many years. Born of an American

36

father and a Swedish mother, he had classic Nordic features. Erect posture, broad shoulders, graceful athleticism—along with a quick wit and hearty laugh, as she recalled. He was also the most generous soul she'd ever known. A man who many women would die for, and others would greedily take advantage of.

Like her former best friend.

Stefan touched her hand. "Awfully glad I was there tonight."

"Why were you? Are you and Monica...?" The woman's name tasted bad in her mouth.

"Guess you haven't heard." He gave a wry laugh and shook his head.

"Don't know if I want to." Penelope turned from him to stare out into the city, taking solace in the dark. She could hardly bring herself to talk about Monica, the woman who'd seduced this exquisite man who stood before her. Penelope chewed her lip thinking about the woman she'd once thought was as close as a sister.

Several years ago, she and Monica were working in southern California when they'd met Stefan after a shoot in San Diego. Monica was more experienced, and so was Stefan, who was wrapping up his Navy SEAL career after returning from Afghanistan. The three of them hung out in the Gaslamp district downtown and went to the beach in the old town of Carlsbad.

A few weeks later, Stefan moved to Los Angeles for law school, where Penelope also had modeling jobs. It wasn't long before they were spending every moment they could together. They dated for one glorious year, with Penelope dashing back to L.A. every chance she had and Stefan studying hard while she was gone.

On one trip, while Penelope was on a shoot in New York, their idyllic existence was suddenly torn apart like palm fronds in a hurricane. She'd just left a job when she found Stefan waiting in the small, marbled lobby of the Elysée Hotel, where she was staying.

"What a nice surprise," she'd said, sliding her arms around his neck and feeling the strange stiffness in his shoulders. "I was just day-dreaming about you… and missing what you do to me."

He'd spoken in a strangled voice. "That's not why I'm here. Let's go to your room. We really have to talk."

Penelope closed her eyes, recalling his confession. She had watched Monica seduce scores of men, so she knew her friend's powers. She knew Monica better than anyone, and was certain that this episode meant nothing to her friend—or to Stefan. *We'll put this behind us and forget it,* that's what she told Stefan when she forgave him, though the knowledge sliced her like a scythe. She'd never been the same since.

"Penelope, are you still with me?"

Blinking, she turned back to him. He was still gripping the railing watching her. She changed the subject. "I know you graduated from USC and joined a prestigious firm. Criminal law, right?"

"I never should have married Monica."

Penelope wanted to scream. "Who held a gun to your head?" she snapped. But she knew the answer. She'd fallen deeply in love with a man so honorable that he couldn't fathom bringing a child into the world and not fulfilling his role as a father.

Two months after Stefan had confessed the brief affair and just as Penelope and Stefan were regaining their relationship, Monica swooped in again.

Pregnant.

Stefan stepped toward her. "Guess I deserved that."

Penelope spun toward him and jabbed him in the chest with a finger. "You got what you deserved. Monica."

Stefan hung his head and rubbed the back of his neck. "It's not enough to say I'm sorry, but I am. What I did was unforgiveable."

Penelope could feel his shame. Somewhere in her heart, she yearned to reach out to comfort him. She'd once loved him, and despite barely surviving the aftermath of her shattered heart, she felt badly for him.

Unable to form words of sympathy, she gripped the railing to thwart her hands and steady her nerves. It'd be so easy to scream at him, to say something to hurt him now, even all these years later, but after tonight, life felt too short to waste another breath on a past that could never be changed.

Tears shone in his eyes, surprising her. "I couldn't leave her after she lost the baby. She was so depressed. She talked of killing herself."

"Of course you couldn't." Penelope forced the words from her throat. "I didn't expect you to."

Stefan touched her hand. "I didn't say I *shouldn't* have left her."

Penelope glanced down, willing her hand to move, but it refused. "Do you have a case in New York?" She had to change the subject. Reliving the past wasn't making this horrible night any better. Penelope wanted to just forget and forge on like she had always done.

Stefan coughed into his hand and took a long swig of acai juice.

Monica had boasted about his career for a while, and then grew bored. *He's working all the time*, Penelope had heard her complain backstage to other models. *He never has time for me.* Penelope saw Monica flirting with other men while they were on location and called her on her behavior, but Monica simply hurled words back in her face. *What business is it of yours?*

Her friend was right. None. So she'd cut her ties to Monica, turning down work that would've brought them together. Thank goodness Penelope's agent had understood and began booking her elsewhere.

Sirens pierced the silence, and Penelope stared at the flashing emergency lights below. Millions of people lived and died in this city. Why should they be any different?

"I'm taking a break from law."

Penelope turned back to Stefan, her lips parted in surprise. "I thought you loved the law. What happened?"

"It's extremely satisfying when I'm representing the good guys and we win. But the practice became tainted. The partners began representing a class of people I found repelling. Mobsters. Child molesters." Stefan ran a hand down her forearm. "The last case did me in. I nearly didn't survive."

Penelope drew her eyebrows together, her instincts on alert. "You survived Afghanistan."

40

"There, we knew who the enemy was." Stefan grimaced and then took her hands in his.

Penelope looked down at their joined hands. Sensing his need for connection and comfort, she made no move to draw back. "Are you going back to law?"

"I don't know when—or if—but I had to do something. So I started a service with a partner that provides premium bodyguards to high profile people. That's why I was at that event. Protecting others is what I do, Penelope. Always has been."

"If you're happy, I'm glad for you, Stefan." She squeezed his hands, reassuring him. Or herself.

Pressing her hands in return, he said, "You really haven't been reading the tabloids, have you?"

"I gave up reading those a long time ago to maintain my sanity." There was no shortage of pairings of her with wildly successful men, playboys, and stars, according to the tabloids and online gossip sites.

"Monica left me for my client."

"Which one?" She frowned. "Not that it matters."

"Oh, it does." He blew out a breath of disgust. "She left me for the actor I got off on murder charges. That was the last case."

Penelope swallowed her shock. "I saw a post on social media, but it was so outlandish, I was certain the story had been fabricated." Overcome with sadness for what he'd been through, she touched his cheek—against her better judgment.

"As it turns out, reality is often stranger than fiction." Stefan slid a finger under her chin. "As you might imagine, I've been reevaluating my life. Despite what I'd thought, I think we have some unfinished business."

Penelope lowered her eyes, containing her desire. "I hardly recall."

He slid his arms around her. "May I refresh your memory?"

3

STEFAN LEANED FORWARD to speak to the driver. "Pull to the curb after the next light."

Penelope shivered in the back seat of the black Town Car. Any other time, she would've enjoyed strolling on an autumn evening in New York, but her nerves were still frazzled after the shooting incident—not to mention the unexpected proximity of Stefan.

"Cold?" he asked, shifting his arm around her. "You're still in mild shock."

She nodded. On several levels. Earlier that evening, her world had shifted on his balcony. This path was dangerous, but she'd faced down threats many times in her career. She could handle it.

Besides, a girl had to eat. Stefan had offered, and really, what could it hurt?

She ran her fingertips over his hand, relishing the feel of his arm around her and remembering what they'd lost so many years ago.

The driver pulled to a stop and Stefan got out first. Satisfied they hadn't been followed, he held his hand out to Penelope and helped her from the car. She'd shed her evening dress and borrowed one of Stefan's long white dress shirts, cinching it at the waist like a dress with a belt and rolling up the sleeves. Thank goodness he was taller than she was.

She still wore her Manolo Blahnik stilettos, but this was New York—where most anything but last year's gown at this year's Met Gala would do. And the more original, the better.

Stefan slid his arm around her. "Is it too soon to say I've missed you?"

"No," she replied, and then added softly, "*Jeg har også savnet dig.*" She quickly turned her face. *I've missed you, too.*

Outside the door, as the scent of garlic wafted through the air, she realized how hungry she was. Glancing at him from the corner of her eye, she admired how he'd taken charge of the evening, though part of her hated to admit it.

Not that she couldn't take care of herself—she had been doing exactly that since she was fourteen. Traveling the world, taking care of friends and family members who needed help, and managing her money so that someday, if she could no longer find modeling work at the ripe old age of thirty or thirty-five, she would have a secure future. Her parents had raised her to be independent and altruistic. It was the Danish way.

A red canopy fluttered above the door. Mama Rosina's was a tiny, living room-sized restaurant tucked between Guido's Shoe Repairs and Lucky Alterations. Penelope knew the best food in New York was often found at tiny neighborhood places. She stepped inside the Italian trattoria and was immediately reminded of the family restaurants she loved to visit whenever she was in Italy. "How'd you find this place?"

"I was out for a run one day when torrential rains forced me to take cover. Smelled so good I couldn't resist. Came back, and the family has been feeding me ever since whenever I'm in town."

"And is that often?"

"More often than not, now. If I hadn't gotten out of L.A. when I did, I would've needed a criminal attorney. Not that Monica knew where the kitchen was located."

As he spoke, a robust man in his fifties with a thick head of white hair crossed the intimate restaurant and held his arms out to them. "Stefan, we've missed you." The two men embraced and exchanged a few words, after which the man showed them to a booth lined with faded burgundy cushions. A woman in a white apron with dark, gray-shot hair knotted in a thick bun—presumably Mama Rosina—waved in welcome from the kitchen. Nearby tables held chattering multigenerational families.

After they sat down, Stefan gazed at her with approval. "You sure do more for that shirt than I do."

"I love it." She flipped up the collar and tilted her nose. "You might not get it back."

"It's yours then. I'll enjoy thinking of you in it." He stretched his arm and rested it on the back of the booth above her shoulders. "Like it here? Pretty different from the fashion show party."

Penelope leaned toward him. His presence was so familiar that she found it easy to fall back into step with him. Too easy, she reminded herself, shifting slightly. "I love intimate places like this where it doesn't matter who you are or where you come from. As long as you're hungry, you're family." Places like this, in the comfortable neighborhood boroughs of New York, were exactly what Penelope liked.

"You won't find any paparazzi or spotlights here."

"I've had enough of that." She shrugged a slim shoulder at this inevitable part of the business. Some models craved the spotlight, though for her, as much as she loved her work, fame had lost its allure. Most days she showed up, did her job, and then went home to remove her makeup, have a swim, and pull on her favorite cotton PJs, although the tabloids often reported otherwise.

Wine and bread soon arrived unbidden. Penelope lifted a glass of fragrant red wine to her nose while admiring the label. "Barolo, very nice, from Piemonte. What are we celebrating?"

He gazed into her eyes. "Tonight, to life." He touched his glass to hers. "Tomorrow, to the future. *Skål*," he added in Danish. *Cheers.*

"*Skål*." Penelope sipped, enjoying the richly nuanced wine, but more than that, she was warming to Stefan's presence. She drank in his strong profile, noting a dusting of gray hair at his temples and subtle, tanned creases at his eyes.

Stefan teased her fingers with his. "Still traveling as much?" he asked, as he looped her pinkie finger with his.

"I'm a gypsy."

"A well paid one, though."

"Fashion Week doesn't pay as well as people think. It's more about the exposure to gain other work. Besides, you never know how long your career will last."

He shifted his arm lower on the booth, gently tapping her shoulder. "How's your schedule these days?"

"As hectic as always." She changed position, brushing his thigh as she did, though she didn't move away. "From September to October, I walk for designers at Fashion Weeks in New York, London, Milan, and Paris. Then it starts all over again in February for the next season's collections."

"Is that all?" He laughed, showing a smile Penelope had always loved.

"Actually, no. I often walk in Paris for the haute couture collections in January and July. Which is how I initially landed my print advertising campaign contracts." Penelope dipped her chin. That's where she made most of her money. "I work hard, but now I can afford to be more discriminating."

"Hope you're banking your funds."

"Of course. Won't last forever. Not when eighteen-year-olds land Chanel No. 5 contracts." She loved traveling, but she lived modestly. She'd bought her home in the Hollywood Hills before the prices had skyrocketed. It was also common practice for a portion of her compensation from designers to be in clothes, so her clothing budget wasn't large.

Stefan nodded, taking in everything she said with an intense expression. "Do you get to see your parents much?"

"Now that they're retired, they travel almost as much as I do, though I visit them in August in Copenhagen when I work that show." She hesitated. "But I'd rather hear about you."

Stefan stroked his chin. "Everyone deserves a fair trial, but I grew tired defending the murderers and rapists feigning innocence."

"That actor. The media branded him as guilty. Was he?"

"In this situation, the media got it right, I'm sure. And I won the case on a brilliant technicality, or so said *Fox News*." He ran a hand over his hair. "Funny, I don't feel so triumphant. I did my job well, but did that really serve society? Or that poor young woman and her family?"

Penelope heard anguish in his voice and saw it in the fall of his shoulders. She'd heard he'd been a star at his law firm. She slid her hand over his, realizing the cost he'd paid to live his dream. "At one time, you wanted to serve those unjustly charged."

"I did that, too. But you can't always choose the cases that land on your desk. Especially those that rack up millions in defense." He paused and took a long sip of wine, his eyes focused on a distant point as his mind reeled back. "You have no idea how gruesome the crime scene was."

She shuddered, imaging how hard it must have been on him, a man of such high principles. "Wasn't it a crime of passion?"

"That was the media spin, and the jury bought it, too. But I don't know if that man has a speck of passion in him. He's cold and calculating. His charm is an act and he's damn good at it." He wagged his head at the memories. "And Monica ran straight into his arms."

"She always thrived on danger."

Stefan gave a sarcastic half-grin. "We both know I wasn't

dangerous enough—or rich enough—for her."

Penelope shifted in the booth next to him, turning toward him. "Then we should be celebrating your divorce."

Swirling the wine in his glass, Stefan frowned. "Divorce—however deserved—always holds sadness. She has some good qualities, but she doesn't let them out often. You know that, Monica was your friend, too."

She shifted uncomfortably in the booth. Monica had been a friend she'd once confided in. She was vivacious and generous, but also crazy envious of anyone she perceived as having more than her. Penelope moistened her lips. Before she let herself slide into his arms again, she had to know more. "Hear from her much?"

"Not until tonight." He drew his eyebrows together in concern. "She saw me and wanted to talk. She seemed desperate, in fact. Guess they broke up."

"And did you?"

"Told I couldn't until later." His eyes dropped to his phone.

"She's been calling, hasn't she?" Penelope had seen him silence his phone a few times.

"There's nothing she has to say that's more important than being here with you. She made her decision." The front door opened with a gust of autumn wind, and Stefan brushed wayward strands of hair from her face. Holding a lock of her hair, he grinned. "I never thought I'd say this, but purple suits you well."

"Don't get too attached. This color won't last long. Never does."

"The rose gold was pretty."

49

Penelope smiled. "Have you been stalking me?"

"It's hard to miss the billboards and television ads."

She'd just finished a lucrative perfume campaign for Dior, her largest one yet. She'd been drenched in rose gold, from her hair to her evening gown. The makeup artist had even covered her skin in rosy golden makeup. "The stylist and photographer had an amazing vision. I'm glad it turned out so well."

"Do you know who else was being considered by the brand?"

Penelope started to shake her head, then parted her lips. "Not..."

"Monica. She smashed up half the house when she found out. And the next day, she was gone."

"She needs help."

"And she has refused it many times. I tried, Penelope. I want you to know that."

"I know you did." Penelope tried to contain the emotions raging within her. It was all she could do to keep from succumbing to his remarkable man. Yet, Monica could be vicious. Toward the end of their friendship, Penelope had watched her take pleasure in torturing people she didn't even care about, just for fun.

A waiter interrupted, delivering a tricolore salad—so named after Italian flag of red, white, and green—with crisp arugula, endive, and radicchio, and studded with plump tomatoes and topped with shaved parmesan.

Penelope smiled. "You remembered."

"Of course." Stefan squeezed her hand. "Your farfalle al salmone is up next. It's not Madeo's in Beverly Hills, but it's as close as I've found in New York."

She kissed him on the cheek. "You really are such a thoughtful man."

"And a superhero, too." He puffed out his chest, teasing her.

"So now you're taking credit?" Playfully, she jabbed him in the chest with her fork.

The owner brought their pasta, and they ate as they caught up, talking about mutual friends and places they'd traveled. Stefan loved the water as much as she did, and he told her about his deep sea fishing trips. When she mentioned a trip to Monaco she'd taken in the spring with a good friend, Dahlia Dubois, to watch the Formula 1 races, he grinned.

"I was there with a client," he said. "That was quite a race. Isn't your friend dating Alain Delamare? I saw photos of them after he won the race."

"You and millions of others." She laughed. "He seems to be a good guy, and they're happy together."

"I hope they are." A shadow crossed Stefan's face.

"While I was there, I helped Dahlia unravel a mystery in her family. We found her mother, reunited her family, and set her history straight." Penelope speared a farfalle.

"You're as fearless as I remember," Stefan said, his eyes lighting with admiration.

"I take action. It's empowering." What she didn't add was that she'd really learned that after the Monica debacle. She'd been hurt more deeply than she'd thought possible.

"I admire your confidence."

Penelope picked up her wine glass and leveled her gaze at him. "Confidence is essential when you prance down the runway in nothing but a lace bustier, six-inch heels, and angel wings."

Stefan nearly choked on a bite of linguine, and the older couple at the next table looked shocked, and then stifled laughter. After gulping a glass of water, he said, "Still doing the Victoria's Secret shows?"

She grinned. "Not anymore." She shrugged a shoulder. "But remember, I'm Danish. We're proud of our bodies. There's nothing shameful about the way we came into this world."

Stefan laughed. "I remember going to a spa in Copenhagen. I think I was the only guy there with a towel. People probably wondered what I was hiding."

Penelope smirked, memories of exactly what he was hiding crossing her mind. "Do you travel often?"

"Most of my work is in L.A., but I send bodyguards all over the world, often on short notice." He twirled pasta onto his fork. "Spend much time in L.A.?"

"Not as much as I'd like. I'm a workaholic."

"So you haven't changed."

"Actually, I'd like to. I'm aging out of runway modeling. My agent is urging me to be more selective, to focus on more lucrative jobs."

Plenty of girls aged fourteen to sixteen would love to take her place in the shows ahead. Most models aged out of runway by twenty-three or twenty-four, though some older models managed to work as long as they could.

Still, she loved meeting her friends on the circuit and showing the season's new styles for the designers she'd grown close to over the years. She was already one of the older models on the catwalk, so she'd been shifting more to commercial print. But even that had a limited time run. It was if models had an expiration date stamped on them. *Best if used by....*

They chatted while they ate, and after dinner, Penelope turned to Stefan. "I have an early call, so I should turn in."

They walked outside to the waiting Town Car. Before he opened the door, Stefan ran a finger along her jawline, and she turned into his hand. "I had a wonderful evening," she said, cradling her cheek in the warmth of his hand.

He brushed his lips across her forehead. "I want to see you again. Under better circumstances," he added. "Just say when."

Penelope's heart thudded. She'd dreamed of hearing these words for so many years. She closed her eyes and let feelings of warmth and love wash over her, just as before. She felt his lips touch hers in a flutter as soft as butterfly wings.

She opened her eyes, taking in the rich details of his face and his penetrating eyes. The intensity of his breathing matched her own. Two hearts, beating in rhythm.

Yet still divided.

"No, please don't call me," she said, her voice strangled.

Stefan's eyes widened with an excruciating expression of disbelief shading his face. He clutched her hands. "You can't mean that."

"I do," she managed to say, her heart splintering.

Stefan pressed his fist to his mouth and opened the rear door for her.

Swinging her long hair to obscure her face, Penelope turned to step into the car before he could see the tears that lined her face.

4

WATCHING THE BLACK Town Car turn the corner, Stefan
expelled a guttural cry and chopped the air with his hand. Why,
of all people, was she involved in this mess?

Acting on a tip, he'd booked this trip to New York to accompany one of his bodyguards assigned to a young star.

That wasn't his usual practice, though. His bodyguards—
men and women—were ex-SEALs, police officers, FBI, martial
artists. They could all take care of themselves and their clients.

The tip he'd received last week had come from an associate
with his old law firm. Sarah Levy was a fellow USC Gould School
of Law graduate, a few years behind him and as smart as they
came. She had asked him to meet her at Nate 'n Al in Beverly
Hills for lunch.

They had started with small talk and after ordering a New
York on rye—hot pastrami, coleslaw, and Russian dressing—
he'd leaned across the deli table. "What's up, Sarah? I'll bet this
isn't a social call. And I know I'm not your type."

"My girlfriend and I are very happy." Her smile had dissolved into a frown of concern. "I have a private investigator on

a case and he came back with information I thought might concern you. I know one of your guys is headed to New York's Fashion Show next week."

Stefan narrowed his eyes. "His wife still in your yoga class?"

"You remembered. Anyway, this is hot." She glanced around the neighboring booths. "One of the tabloid factories is getting creative."

"TMZ?"

"No, another one, but I don't know which one. What I do know is that they want to scoop the news. To be first, they're willing to *create* it."

Stefan drummed a finger on the Formica tabletop. "How exactly?"

"They're setting up celebrities, then running with the stories."

"So someone is caught in a compromising position. What's new about that?"

"This is much bigger than that. They're looking for explosive headlines. How, I don't know, but from what I heard, there was a lot of money exchanging hands."

"Where'd your man get this info?"

"Said he overheard a guy boasting about it in a bar. But something big is going to happen at Fashion Week in New York. I thought you'd want to know so that your bodyguard could take extra precautions. Don't tell him it came from me. His wife is worried enough as it is."

"Course not." He asked a few more questions as they ate, but Sarah couldn't provide any other details.

After he had left the restaurant, he'd made immediate arrangements for New York.

What he hadn't known was that Penelope was giving a talk at the venue. He could only assume that she was the target of the scheme that Sarah had told him about.

And now, tonight, he'd had his chance with Penelope, and he'd blown it.

Stefan strode to his apartment, hoping the cool air would clear his heated mind, but it did little good. Monica had come between them, and he'd made his choice. To this day, he still wondered how he'd become so drunk that he hadn't remembered asking Monica to his apartment.

Cutting across the street, he thought of Penelope. He still remembered the hurt in her eyes when he'd told her about Monica.

Would he ever have another chance with Penelope? There was so much he'd wanted to say to her over dinner, but after what she'd been through today, he couldn't bring himself to cause her any more distress. Stupidly, he had done next to nothing.

As he neared his apartment, the smell of broiled hot dogs teased his nose. He sidestepped a small crowd gathered around a street meat vendor. Just then, his phone buzzed in his pocket, and he pulled it out.

A message from an unknown number flashed on his screen. *Missed her this time.*

Frowning, Stefan tapped a reply. *Who's this?* While he waited, he checked the number, and screen snapped a photo of the message and number. It was an overseas number, probably routed through a back door to reach him.

Nothing.

He jabbed the screen to call the number. As he suspected, he received an automated message saying the number was out of order.

Sarah's warning rushed back to him. Someone was taunting him. Someone who had access to sophisticated equipment and networks. Not a rogue photographer or fan as the police imagined. No, the event tonight was a concerted effort. The lights were cut, allowing the perpetrator to get away. At least two people were involved, probably more. A cybercrime. He checked his phone. A chill bristled on his neck. He had to warn Penelope, but he hadn't even gotten her number. And he'd have to change his now.

He tapped a call he'd made earlier. "This is Stefan Armstrong," he said. "The car I booked this evening, where is it headed now?" The driver had already dropped Penelope off at her hotel.

"Which hotel?" Listening, he nodded, then hung up and tapped another number.

"Penelope Plessen's room, please."

A short silence ensued. "There's no one here by that name."

He rubbed his forehead. What name had she used in the past? "Try Elizabeth Bennet." She'd been a huge Jane Austen fan at one time.

"Hold for Ms. Bennet's room, please."

Stefan waited, trying to quell his anxiety.

"Hello?"

He let out a breath. "Penelope, I just called to make sure you got back to your hotel okay."

"Stefan? How did you know where I'm staying?"

"The car service."

The line was quiet for a moment. "If I didn't know you better, I'd think you were stalking me."

Stefan banged his hand against his forehead. What a creepy thing he'd done, but he had to make sure she was safe.

"Get any other calls?"

"No-o." Penelope drew out the word.

Should he tell her? "Be careful, Penelope. I have reason to believe you may be in danger."

"You called to tell me that?" She sounded weary and angry. "Because a man fired a shot at me today, so I think I can figure that out on my own."

"Penelope—"

"I asked you not to call me."

"And I respect that, but—"

"Goodnight, Stefan."

The line went dead. Despite her words, he could hear the hurt in her voice. Stefan punched the air in frustration. Not only was he worried about her, but he was sure she'd been crying. In all the years he'd been married to Monica, he'd heard her scream and rant, threaten and cajole, but never, ever had she cried.

The sound of Penelope's voice broke his heart. What had she ever done to him but love him so completely that now she couldn't stand to be near him? He'd beat himself up over this for years. How could he have been so weak in a moment that Monica

59

actually looked like a better option? He wished he could recall that night, but all he remembered was waking up with Monica.

No question, he owed Penelope a debt for having jilted her in the worst possible way. Yet he couldn't erase the past, so the least he could do for her now was to protect her when she needed it. Even if she wouldn't let him.

The next morning, he awoke to a phone call. "Stefan here."

"Jack. Got some news."

It was Johann Jackovich, the bodyguard for the young star at the party last night. "How's our client?"

"Fine. No problem there. This is about that model, Penelope Plessen. The one you took off the stage. Thought you might want to know this."

"Spill it," he said, sitting up and swinging his legs off the bed.

"She disappeared from her hotel room last night. It's all over the news this morning."

Stefan bolted up and grabbed his jeans. "Thanks, gotta go, Jack."

5

Los Angeles, California

"WHAT BRINGS YOU here so early, Penelope?" Lance Martel held the back door to the restaurant open for her.

"Just stepped off a plane at LAX. It's good to see you." Penelope gave him a hug. Lance was wearing his white chef's jacket and smelled of a delicious mixture of spices—rosemary, garlic, and oregano—which reminded her that she hadn't eaten since New York.

"My best girlfriend and Scarlett are at a table in the back. Go on through. I'm making breakfast for you all now."

"You're a sweetheart, thanks." Penelope walked into the dining room of Bow-Tie, a popular bistro in Beverly Hills that her friends Lance and Johnny had started. She wore a gray scarf over her hair and dark sunglasses. Her face was scrubbed clean of last night's makeup, but she still wore Stefan's white shirt belted as a dress, though she had managed to trade her Manolo Blahniks for a pair of Nikes at an airport shop. Her jeweled shoes were nestled in a black canvas tote bag she'd bought, along with makeup re-mover, moisturizer, and lip gloss. All the essentials in less than ten minutes to boarding time.

Two blond women in yoga gear motioned for her to join them at their table.

"Verena, Scarlett, I'm so glad you could meet me." Penelope hugged her friends and slid into a chair with her back to the room. Penelope used to have facials at a skincare salon Verena had owned, and she'd appeared in infomercials for Verena's new skincare line as a favor to help her new venture, which had since proven quite successful.

"We heard all about it on the news," Verena said, her voice ringing with compassion. Her hair was pulled back into a loose ponytail, revealing her flawless complexion. "How awful that must've been. We're so relieved you weren't hurt. Did you know the photographer?"

"Never saw him before." Penelope quickly filled them in. "After I returned to my hotel, I lay on the bed thinking about what I'm doing with my life. Why am I working at such a frenetic pace? I could have been killed yesterday."

"Surely they'll find the guy," Scarlett said, her tone serious. Scarlett Sandoval was Penelope's licensing attorney and had drafted the High Gloss Cosmetics agreement for her.

"Hope so." Penelope slid off her sunglasses. "It gets worse. Last night I couldn't sleep, so I went down to the bar for a glass a wine, and was chatting with the bartender when a photographer started snapping away just outside the window."

"Someone at the hotel tipped them off."

"I don't think so. I've stayed there for years and the staff is very discreet. Someone on the street might have recognized me." She grimaced. "So I went outside to confront him, and when I did, another guy grabbed me."

"What happened?" Verena asked, frowning with concern.

"I got away." Penelope held up a bruised hand. "That guy's probably icing his nose somewhere."

"I'm so sorry. We'll get some ice for you, too." Verena signaled a busboy who was placing flowers on the tables.

Penelope went on. "I thought to myself, what am I doing here, brawling on the streets in New York? And that lousy photographer was snapping away. By morning, I knew the press would be camped outside, so I dashed out through the employee entrance, caught a cab, and went straight to the airport to catch an overnight flight home."

Scarlett touched her arm. "What do you need from us?"

"Can you take me back to my house?" After two incidents in one day, she was nervous now. "I don't know what I'll find there."

Verena and Scarlett traded looks of concern. "If you want to wait until after lunch, maybe Lance or Johnny could come with you," Scarlett said. "Or we can come with you right now."

"The sooner the better. I have to push back a photo shoot for High Gloss and make some calls."

"What about Fashion Week?" Scarlett asked. "Aren't you walking in some shows?"

Penelope pulled out her phone and tapped on a message.

The busboy delivered a plastic bag of ice, and she rested her injured hand against it while Verena and Scarlett read the note from her agent.

"Your gigs were canceled?" Scarlett frowned as she read the message.

"Seems so." Penelope sighed. "Saw this when I got back to my hotel, so I called her. Designers started canceling my contracts soon after the shot was fired. None of them want trouble at their shows, so they cut me." And she hadn't even told them about Stefan.

Verena looked incredulous. "They can do that?"

Scarlett shrugged. "I'm sure there's a clause in the contract that addresses things like that. Designers spend a fortune on their shows. They can't risk a disruption."

"Until that guy is caught, I'm off the runway." A split second was all it took to derail the career she'd nurtured so carefully. One shot that splintered a podium, and she was verboten, banned, taboo. Who was he and why had he singled her out? On the flight from New York, she'd tried to recall if she'd ever seen the man who'd tried to kill her, but she couldn't think of anything.

"Hope you're hungry." Lance placed a skillet with a vegetable frittata in front of them, while Johnny followed with a pot of coffee and a basket of croissants and rolls.

"Thanks, babe," Verena said, giving Lance a kiss.

Penelope watched them, happy that they were getting along so well. Scarlett was also dating Johnny, Lance's partner in Bow-Tie, who handled everything but the kitchen. His thick, dark hair was swept back and he wore a polka-dotted bow-tie, his trade-mark look he'd adopted while he was working as a maître d' at the Polo Lounge, and the inspiration for the restaurant name.

Johnny gave Penelope a hug. "Sorry to hear about that mess in New York." He shifted from one foot to the other. "I don't mean to alarm you, but have you checked out social media lately?"

"Not since last night, why?"

Johnny pulled out his phone. "It seems you've been kid-napped from your hotel and police are searching for you."

"*What?*" Penelope tapped his phone. "These are the photos from last night in front the hotel."

"Look at this one." Lance peered over her shoulder. "Good hit, Penelope. Right into the nose, ouch. Where'd you learn that move?"

"I do Krav Maga training on the west side." She stretched out her aching palm.

Johnny looked impressed. "That's the Israeli work-out, isn't it?"

Penelope nodded. "It's derived from the Israeli Defense Force training. And evidently it's pretty effective."

"I'll say." Scarlett leaned in, squinting. "It says you were ab-ducted in that van." She enlarged the photo. "Look, there's no license plate on the back. That was staged."

"Who's doing this to me?" Penelope passed a weary hand across her face.

Scarlett folded her arms in disgust. "And why?"

"Listen to this." In between bites of the frittata, Verena

flipped through her phone. She began reading the headlines. "*Monica Blackburn to Strut in Kidnapped Supermodel's Shoes at Fashion Week. And, Prime Minister Shattered over Supermodel's Disappearance.*"

"That last one's a lie." Penelope leaned back, stunned. What had Stefan said about Monica going ballistic over a job she'd lost to her? Even for Monica, this seemed extreme. "No way is Monica smart enough to pull off a stunt like this."

Scarlett tore a croissant and nibbled it, thinking. "Who else stands to gain?" When everyone stopped to look at her, she added, "Someone has gone to a lot of trouble. Why?"

Johnny jerked his head toward the front door. "Don't look now, but we've got paparazzi at the door. Little early for them. We don't open for lunch for a couple of hours yet."

"I can guess why they're here," Penelope said. "I just want to go home." It felt like the world was closing in on her.

Scarlett touched Verena's hand. "Let's get her out of here now."

"Then this order is to go." Lance scooped up the croissants and rolls in a linen napkin and handed it to Verena. "Take her out the back."

Scarlett stood. "I've also got to call the police to let them know you're okay."

Verena put a hand to her mouth. "That's all we need is to be arrested for kidnapping you."

"You ladies better make tracks," Johnny said. "Follow me."

The three women darted through the busy kitchen to the back door. Johnny pushed open the door and held it for them.

Lance pressed the car remote and tossed his keys to Verena. "Take my SUV. The windows are darkened."

Penelope swung past him. "Really? Do this often?"

"It's for catering jobs. Protects food from the sunlight." Lance held the car doors for them.

Verena slid into the driver's seat, and Scarlett climbed into the passenger side, while Penelope stretched out in the backseat. They buckled their seatbelts and turned into the alley.

"It's blocked," Verena said, spotting a van at the end of the alley. She checked the review mirror. "That side, too." Turning around in her seat, she motioned to Penelope. "You'd better get down."

They passed the media van at the end of the alley and drove on through the busy streets of Los Angeles, while Penelope tried to reach her agent. Verena drove north on Fairfax into the Hollywood Hills, but when she turned onto Penelope's street, she slowed to a halt. Media vans lined the narrow lane.

"What the hell?" Penelope peered through the windshield along high hedges and walls other neighbors had built for privacy and protection.

Scarlett glanced back at Penelope. "Looks like you have company."

"I just want to have a swim and sleep in my own bed."

"You can cross off swimming. I'm sure they have cameras dangling over your wall. Now what?"

Penelope felt overwhelmed. She just needed a place to rest and shower. She'd left New York so fast she hadn't even packed. The hotel staff was kind enough to send her luggage back for her.

"How about your place?"

Verena shifted the SUV into reverse and eased out of the narrow street.

"Why not?" Scarlett replied with a grin. "The neighbors will love this."

Feeling grateful, Penelope closed her eyes. She wondered if the media would follow her to Scarlett's. Though she appreciated the gesture, she couldn't subject Scarlett to a media circus, either. This was L.A.; it might be only a matter of time before someone tipped off the press.

If she couldn't go home, then where could she go to rest and avoid the media attention? She thought back to her childhood, to carefree days of fishing with her father or skiing with her parents. At the time, she hadn't thought to appreciate the tranquility and anonymity she'd enjoyed in Denmark. If she had to, what were the chances she could recapture some of that and take a breather there?

As Scarlett whipped down Fairfax and turned onto Beverly, Penelope peered out the window behind them. Her heart sank as she recognized a van that had been parked on her street tailing them.

6

Copenhagen, Denmark

PENELOPE STRETCHED IN her business class seat aboard a
Scandinavian SAS flight, her head still throbbing with stress. The
seat reclined flat and the ten-hour flight was the first time she'd
slept since before she'd left New York. Touching a button that
elevated her seat, she reached for a bottle of water and drank,
thankful for the predawn quietness in the shrouded cabin. Few
people other than flight attendants were awake at this hour.

Penelope enjoyed the solitude of flying, particularly after the
last two days. After being unable to get past the paparazzi to her
home in peace, she had been followed to Scarlett's townhouse in
the SUV that Verena drove. In less than a day, the media attention had become a nightmare that Penelope felt she couldn't im-
pose on friends.

Never mind the social media and tabloid accounts of the
event in New York. She'd been linked to countless actors, a Prime
Minister, and a Greek billionaire. She didn't even know half the
people she was supposedly dating. Now, a worldwide search was

on for her, and conjuncture about her Russian and underworld ties were being spun in the tabloids. Most of it wasn't even remotely true.

Except for the Greek billionaire. Kristo Demopoulos had made his fortune not in shipping, but in software that controlled and optimized shipping processes around the world. He was a modern day Onassis. They'd met in Monaco, and he'd been interested in her, but she'd been in recovery from Stefan. Though they'd never dated, she seemed to run into Kristo often, and had watched his transformation from star-stuck software geek to billionaire.

Before she decided what she was going to do about her tattered life, she was going home. Her family kept an apartment in the old section of Copenhagen. She loved her native country, but she'd been gone so long she felt like a tourist now in Denmark. Her memory of the cobble-stoned streets had dimmed, and many places she'd known as a child had changed. She prayed she could find some semblance of quiet anonymity there.

Recalling recent events, she felt so grateful for her friends. They had all rallied around her—Fianna, Elena, and Davina in New York. Scarlett, Verena, Lance, and Johnny in L.A.

And even, she had to admit, Stefan. She sighed and took another sip of water. Part of her aching head was undoubtedly related to him.

A week ago, her life had been busy and normal, planning her next jobs with her agent and assistant, swimming and going to Krav Maga classes, and jetting off to her next work location. She lived out of a suitcase most of the year, so her cottage that clung to the side of a cliff in the Hollywood Hills had been her respite from the world. Now that it had been staked out by media vans, she could no longer carry on life as she knew it.

First her runway work, then her home. She thought of conversations she'd once had about mythology with her father. Was she like Icarus, who had flown too close to the sun? She took another drink of water to clear her mind. What could possibly happen next?

Around her, passengers were beginning to stir as the flight attendants wheeled trolleys with coffee and juice down the narrow aisle. Penelope thought about what lay ahead for her. For years, she and friends had planned trips—snow skiing or spas—in between her work demands to have fun, unwind, and plan their lives. She had always looked forward to these adventures, which were filled with friendship and positive planning.

As she was booking her flight for Copenhagen, she thought about her friends and who might like to join her. If they could avoid the media spotlight, which she thought possible in Denmark. So she'd asked Verena and Scarlett, and texted invitations to her other closest friends. Only Elena, who was still in New York, said she could meet her.

Penelope was still waiting to hear from Dahlia, who had been traveling in France with her grandmother Camille while seeing to their perfume businesses. She'd done commercial modeling work for Camille's Parfums Dubois in the past, but now she doubted she'd have much business with the company until this scandal blew over, unless Camille chose to support her despite it.

As the flight attendants passed, a middle-aged female passenger tiptoed behind them and slipped a small notebook and a pen onto Penelope's tray table. "Would you mind giving me your autograph? I've been following the awful shooting and kidnapping in New York."

"As you can see, I wasn't really kidnapped." Penelope managed a wan smile and scribbled her name across the page for the American woman. "But thank you for your concern."

"You live such an exciting life. This is my first visit overseas."

Exciting wasn't how Penelope would describe the last two days of her life, but she supposed that living vicariously might have its thrills. "I hope you enjoy your stay."

The woman leaned closer to her. "How did you manage to escape your kidnappers?"

Hadn't the woman heard her? "It was all a media hoax."

The woman drew the corners of her mouth down in disappointment. "I don't understand. Who was behind it?"

"I wish I knew. It's caused me a lot of anxiety."

The woman shook her head. "My husband always told me that I couldn't trust my little newspapers, but I told him they couldn't possibly print stories that weren't true. And they're so much more interesting than regular newspapers." She scrunched up her brow. "But it was also on the Internet."

"Yes, I know," Penelope said with a sigh.

"That's just not right," the woman said with sudden conviction. "Such lies."

"Be careful what you read." She took the woman's hand. "Copenhagen is special. I hope you enjoy it."

After landing, when Penelope exited customs, she heard her name called. Crestfallen, she slid her gaze toward the person who'd called out.

"Penelope, it's me, Elena. Over here."

"I'm so relieved it's you," she said, hugging the slim brunette she'd last seen at the party in New York.

Elena clamped her hand over her mouth. "I shouldn't have called out your name." She glanced around, but no one paid them any attention. "Maybe we should give you a code name until all this blows over. You know, like 007 or something."

Penelope couldn't help but laugh, and then realized it had been days since she'd felt like laughing. "I'm not a spy."

"But you are a hunted woman." Elena rolled her eyes. "You have no idea about the paparazzi that was gathered outside Davina's apartment in New York."

"I hate you had to go through that."

"Oh, God, it's not *your* fault." Elena put her hand on her hip. "You should have seen Davina handle them, calling them pox and bollix and who knows what other Irish insults before they moved on, their tails between their legs. I've never seen anyone hurl curse words with such class. Reminded me of an old Maureen O'Hara film I once saw."

Penelope had a few choice lines of her own that Davina would surely enjoy. "Who do you think she learned it from?"

Elena's eyes widened. "What, really?"

"They were friends, though Davina was younger. You should hear the stories."

"That's us in thirty years," Elena said, laughing.

Penelope grinned. "Don't you know it."

"It's adorable," Elena said, spinning around the cozy apartment that looked out over a cobble-stoned street lined with flower boxes.

"This was my grandmother's flat," Penelope said, opening windows to let the fresh sea air in. She glanced up and down the street and thankfully, didn't see any paparazzi. "My parents live outside the city, but they keep this place for trips and visitors. When they're away, I like to stay here because it's close to everything."

"I might never leave," Elena said, laughing. "Where do you want to go first?"

"Copenhagen is an easy city to navigate," Penelope said. She was glad she'd invited Elena. Otherwise, she might have hidden inside the apartment for days. She peered outside at the quiet street. "We can walk along the Strøget, a long pedestrian boulevard, and have lunch and do some shopping."

Penelope flung her tote bag on the bed in the blue-and-white bedroom with polished wooden floors. Since she hadn't been home, she was still traveling light, though she had picked up some jeans and T-shirts in the airport, and restocked her cosmetics at the duty free shops.

Leaning against the window, Penelope looked out from the side, breathing in the cool air from the sea. Best of all, there were no paparazzi, no photographers, no media. Just quiet, ordinary people walking past or riding bikes. Pure bliss.

Along Strøget, Elena and Penelope found lots of shops from all around the world, as well as many that were uniquely Danish. They started with coffee at Café Europa looking out over a large square and afterward shopped at Sand and Mads Nørgaard for modern minimalist styles. They strolled through Georg Jensen admiring sleek silverware and jewelry, and stopped in local artisan's shops for soft sweaters against the evening chill.

Penelope chatted with some of the shopkeepers in Danish. Though she missed being here, she'd been gone so long that the city had changed. Things weren't the same as she'd recalled. And now, people treated her differently. You could never really go home, she decided.

They had lunch outdoors at Café Norden, sharing a seasonal salad, fish, and a cheese board while they watched people walking by and talked about different styles they observed. There, Penelope felt a prickly sensation on the back of her neck, as though she were being watched, but she shrugged it off.

Elena wanted to visit Marianne Dulong, a pair of goldsmiths and jewelry designers she admired for their smooth, fluid lines. After that, Penelope took her to Nyhavn, where rows of 17th and 18th century townhomes splashed in ochre, mustard, and sky blue were rivaled by colorful vessels moored steps away from outdoor cafés on the canal.

Looking behind her first, Penelope stopped in front of one and looked up, shielding her eyes from the sun. "One of Denmark's most beloved storytellers lived in that one," she said, pointing to a window. "Remember *The Little Mermaid* and *Thumbelina*?"

Elena smiled. "Hans Christian Andersen. One of my favorites."

Later that evening, they went to a restaurant Penelope recalled from her visits, Frk. Barners Kælder. "So, what do you think of Copenhagen?" Penelope asked Elena over dinner. The stone walls and red-checkered tablecloths created a cozy atmosphere Penelope enjoyed, as well as the traditional food she'd missed. Skagen toast with shrimp, herring, and salmon—she loved the variety.

"The flat is charming, the food delicious, and the company is the best. What's not to like?" Elena cradled her chin in her hand. "The jewelry designs are intriguing, too. Lots of spare, elegant designs with smooth lines. And many avant-garde pieces. Thanks for inviting me."

"I'm awfully glad you could come." Though she'd traveled the world on her own, the more Penelope thought about what had happened in New York, the more wary she was becoming. It was one thing to deal with the media focus that came with her job, but the threat of a violent stalker was unnerving. Had the man been caught? She was relieved to be out of New York, though she still didn't feel like she was out of danger, and she couldn't shake the feeling that she was being followed. Was it just nerves?

She pulled her attention back to Elena. "Where do you find inspiration for your designs?" Penelope asked, slicing a broiled potato with rosemary.

"The sea in all its aspects inspires me. Reminds me of growing up in Sydney." Elena touched her swirled earrings in ribbed gold. "Smooth, undulating forms of water and sand…bold, powerful statements of the sea, and rich colors and textures of the coral reef and marine life. Jewelry and nature…rainbows of stones, gold and silver, it's all found in nature, like the red coral in this bracelet." She slipped off her bracelet and handed it to Penelope to see.

"This new line with the bezel-set stones is stunning," Penelope said, trying on the wide bracelet. "Looks like this piece required a lot of work. I love coral with turquoise for the summer."

"Exactly. I've also worked yellow jade and lemon citrine into some pieces to reflect the sun. I like the spare Danish design aesthetic, and I've seen a lot of ocean influence. Denmark has such a vibrant coastal area."

They were immersed in a discussion about design trends when a waiter interrupted them with a pair of small aperitif glasses. "Another patron thought you might like our lavender-infused Aquavit."

"Aquavit, what's that?" Elena asked.

"It's a traditional aperitif," Penelope said. "It's usually flavored with caraway or cardamom. Careful, it's fairly strong." She lifted the tulip-shaped glass to her nose and inhaled the familiar scent. "Who shall we thank?" she asked the waiter.

The waiter nodded to man in the corner who sat by himself. The man waved at them.

"Kristo," she said and smiled, motioning for him to join them.

The trim, dark-haired man with an intense expression joined them at their table, exchanging cheek kisses with Penelope and

Elena.

"Penelope, I knew we were destined to meet again soon," Kristo said. "I always think of you when I visit Copenhagen, so imagine my surprise when I saw you and your friend walk in." His dark, deep set eyes roved approvingly over her. "Purple suits you. Looks good in photographs, too."

Penelope shifted in her chair, avoiding his penetrating gaze. "Elena, this is Kristo Demopoulos. We met in Monaco a couple of years ago."

"Enchanted," he said, executing an air kiss over Elena's hand before turning to her.

"The last couple of days I've heard some awful news about you. Is this true?" In his eagerness he leaned in, almost too near Penelope's face.

Penelope moved to one side and sighed. "Part of it is." She went on to explain a little, but she was tired of going over the incident. "I'm sorry you were pulled into the stories, too. Do you mind if we talk about something else?" It had been months since Penelope had any contact with Kristo, and she was embarrassed that he had been dragged through the tabloids because of her. She came to Copenhagen to get away from everything, not to rehash it.

"Not at all." He slid his hand awkwardly over hers. "I didn't mean to upset you, but I worry about you. Have you been getting my texts?"

Penelope shook her head. "I got a new number a few months ago."

Kristo whipped out his phone. "What is it?"

Penelope shot a look at Elena and hesitated. It wasn't that she didn't want to give Kristo her new number, but after the last few days, she was afraid to trust anyone outside her closest friends.

When Penelope wasn't quick to respond, Kristo added, "I'm throwing a huge launch party in L.A. for a new product soon. I want to invite you and your friends."

Though attending any party was the last thing on her to-do list, she couldn't deny Kristo's eager smile. Acquiescing, she gave him her number.

Penelope lifted the aperitif to her lips. "This has a wonderful aroma." She said to Elena, "Do you know about Linje Aquavit?"

"I just asked the waitress to bring you something interesting." Kristo drew his chair closer to Penelope. "Linje. Doesn't that mean line?"

"It refers to the equatorial line," Penelope said. "Stored in kegs deep in the bowels of ships, Aquavit crosses the equatorial line twice on its way to and from Australia. The rocking motion and maritime humidity gives the liquor a unique flavor that can't be matched. Then the kegs are tapped and the Aquavit is bottled. It's our Danish tradition to enjoy it at Christmas." She raised her glass. "Skål."

"That's a clever story," he replied. "I'll have to remember that. And check my ships for kegs."

"You have ships?" Penelope had often thought about what she'd do after modeling. The more successful models knew how to maximize their limited time in the industry. "I thought you'd created shipping software."

"Business has been so good that I needed to diversify my holdings. Shipping makes sense, among other things. But I have something extra special I've been working on. I think you'll like it."

Penelope deflected the intensity of his gaze. Kristo had become more attractive since she'd first met him—he'd had quite a drastic physical and financial makeover, in fact, from software geek to billionaire—but she still wasn't interested. She even felt a little sorry for him because of his awkward social graces. "What other types of business have you invested in?"

Kristo held her gaze. "Media and entertainment."

Elena perked up at that mention. "Where?"

"The company is based in New York. It covers the entire U.S. and other counties."

"What's attractive about that business?" Penelope asked, curious about his choice.

"The financials." Kristo continued to stare at her. "It's amazing how much content people consume. And it's growing worldwide." He cocked his head. "How do you keep up with what's going on in the world?"

"On my phone, mostly." Elena leaned forward. "But I admit to spending way too much time on social media and following celebrities. In my work, I have to know who's wearing what."

Kristo shifted his gaze to Elena. "You're not alone. Celebrity news is big business. Headlines sell click-throughs and advertisers pay for eyeballs."

Penelope frowned into her aperitif. "Judging from the media frenzy I've endured since that incident in New York, I get it."

Kristo sipped his liquor. "You should take time to enjoy life. See the world. You could come with me."

The conversation was making Penelope uneasy. Her phone buzzed and she drew it out of her bag. Glancing down, she frowned at the message, tapped a quick reply, and then shut off her phone.

Elena leaned over, concern etched on her face. "Are you okay?"

"More cancellations." Penelope didn't add that media outlets were clamoring for interviews. When would this incident die so she could have her normal life back?

"Remember what Andy Warhol said." Kristo touched her hand, his dark, deep set eyes flashing. "In media time, you've got fifteen minutes to succeed, or fail. What are you going to do with it?"

Could her career crash that quickly? A chill spiraled down Penelope's spine.

"Take a break," Kristo said. "Come and cruise with me on my new yacht tomorrow. Both of you."

"Really? Oh, wow, we'd love to," Elena said, her brown eyes warming to the idea. "I've never actually been on a yacht before."

Penelope gave a wan smile. "Sure, why not?" Elena was curious and she's traveled a long way. She sipped her drink, listening as Elena asked questions about Kristo's yacht.

Kristo really wasn't so bad. She couldn't think of an excuse to avoid him, but after the close calls she'd had in New York and the media circus in L.A., her senses were now on high alert. Those were the only reasons she could think of as to why the skin on her neck now seemed to crawl with apprehension.

7

ELENA FLOPPED ONTO the bed in the apartment. "Stefan, Kristo, wow. How many other sexy exes are you hiding?"

"I never actually dated Kristo, but according to tabloids, there are a whole lot more," Penelope said, checking the street below. She was growing obsessive about her privacy, however, the street seemed clear. She turned to Elena. "Wish I knew half of them."

Raising herself on her elbows, Elena asked, "If you had to choose, which one would you take? I'll take the other one."

Penelope slipped off her shoes, smirking at her friend. "Neither. Stefan was married to a friend of mine, and Kristo is obsessive. Didn't you notice?" She'd told Elena about Stefan and Monica at lunch.

Elena rolled over on the bright blue-and-white Marimekko floral bedspread. "You still call Monica a friend? She broke the girl code in the worst way possible."

Penelope pulled a silk nightie from a drawer. "He made his choice."

"She lied," Elena replied, resting her chin in her hands and glaring. "I would've been absolutely devo."

Penelope laughed at Elena's down-under slang. "I *was* devastated." Penelope recalled how angry, hurt, and anguished she'd been. "I was furious with Stefan, but I knew Monica and had seen her play games. Underneath it all, she was really insecure. Her family was never supportive of her dreams—quite the opposite. Her family split when she was a baby, her mother had a prescription drug habit, and her dad disappeared. She was bullied at school because of her height."

Elena shook her head. "None of that is an excuse for her behavior. She violated a sacred friendship vow: Thou shalt not steal the other's boyfriend."

"It takes two, you know." Penelope punched a pillow. "I blame Stefan just as much." She picked up a hairbrush from the vanity, and then perched on the bed. "Still, I couldn't believe she'd done that to me, her closest friend. When that happened, I lost two of my closest relationships at once."

Elena cradled her chin in her hand. "That sucked. Ever talk to her?"

"I might have a soft heart, but I'm not stupid." Penelope shook out her hair, thinking as she brushed it. When she'd seen Monica at the event in New York, she'd had a strange feeling about her. She couldn't define it, but Monica had avoided eye contact, as though she were hiding something, and wiggled her leg nervously. It was more like Monica to grin and gloat.

Penelope's phone buzzed, and she glanced at the text. "My agent is trying to fill the vacancies on my schedule. Looks like I have a cover shoot for a small beauty magazine that's distributed in Scandinavia."

"That's good, isn't it?"

Penelope shrugged. "It's always good to have work." This gig was a big step down for her, so she knew her agent was hustling to find anything for her. She might be on top, but she wasn't a prima donna. She tapped her reply, accepting the shoot.

The next morning dawned with the sun peeking through the shuttered windows. Penelope flung them open to clear azure skies.

"It's a gorgeous day to be on the water," Penelope called out to Elena. She chose a turquoise Pucci print bikini with a cover up, topping off her ensemble with a broad-brimmed straw hat and white Tom Ford sunglasses.

"Great sunnies," Elena said, stepping from the shower.

Penelope grinned. "Ta," she said, thanking Elena. She loved her friend's Australian vernacular and how she shortened a lot of words. Being around her so often, she'd picked up quite a few things.

Elena smiled and pulled out a sleek black Trina Turk swimsuit with a sheer black cover-up and bronze-colored sandals. She added gold earrings she'd designed and wound her hair into a loose bun. "What do you think?"

"Very chic."

After bathing and dressing, Penelope peered out over the window box filled with red gardenias. "Kristo's pulling up." He was driving a candy red Bentley Supersports Continental convertible. When he glanced up, she waved to signal him. "We'll be right down," she called out. He looked so happy to see them that she felt bad for thinking about how geeky he could be.

Elena peered around her. "Wow, what a ride. That'll attract some attention."

"Kristo likes expensive toys and churns through them with surprising speed. And you look gorgeous today, so be careful around that one."

Elena winked at her. "My aunt always said a woman could fall in love with a wealthy man as easily as a poor one."

"Just be sure to look beneath the fancy exterior," Penelope said, poking her in the ribs.

"Oh, champers, ta," Elena said, accepting a glass of champagne from a server.

"What a beautiful vessel." Penelope ran her hand along a sleek railing aboard the glittering white yacht.

Kristo beamed. "She's brand new. A two-hundred-thirteen feet Manta Explorer. Designed by the Dutch, built in Italy. A real jewel." His eyes gleaned, beholding the thrill of his acquisition.

Penelope recognized his expression though, and knew that when the buzz of newness wore off, he'd be on to his next conquest. She thought back to her childhood, when summers meant accompanying her father and uncle on fishing vessels that lacked luxury but offered a young girl all the excitement of high seas adventure. She missed those days. Why was it she hadn't appreciated those simple times when she'd had them?

They had lunch outside as they cruised. Afterward, Kristo picked up a tablet and flicked it on. "You've got to see my latest project." The tablet lit up and he tapped the screen. "Look at this. It's going to be the highest-selling game of all time."

Fascinated, Penelope looked on. She hadn't known he was interested in gaming, but he had started as a software engineer. He'd once been super geeky, but after his company went public, he'd hired a trainer and a stylist and morphed into a new version designed to attract women, though there was still something odd about him.

Penelope squinted. "Wait a minute. That looks like me." An unsettling feeling crept up her neck.

Kristo grinned. "Gamers can upload photos and turn their players into miniature versions of whoever they like. Now anyone can be a master of the universe."

"That's kind of creepy," Elena said, watching a mini-version of a scantily-clad Penelope warrior battling a dragon.

"Come on," Kristo said. "Why should only the wealthy have all the fun?" He leaned toward them conspiratorially. "Look, a small number of powerful people control the entire world. This way, gamers can control the world they create with whatever characters they want, just like the big boys. Great technology, right?"

"What do you mean, a small number of people?" Penelope asked.

"Don't be so naïve," Kristo said, ticking off his fingers. "Software, media, transportation, food. A few world leaders and their friends run the show."

Penelope and Elena exchanged a glance. "Are you one of those friends?" Penelope asked.

A smug look crossed Kristo's face. He tilted his chair back and crossed his arms, his eyes glittering with delight. "What do you think?"

Penelope was quickly growing tired of this game. "Now you're just showing off."

"Isn't that what you do?" He laughed. "With enough connections and control of the media, anyone can be made—or broken. Common people don't even know they're being played." Kristo stood. "Excuse me. I have to speak to the captain. Look around if you'd like. There's a Jacuzzi on the next deck." He hesitated. "But don't go too far. I have remodeling in progress on a lower deck." He strode from the deck and disappeared below.

Elena watched him go. "Pretty sure of himself. And that's just bizarre," she added, nodding toward the tablet he'd left behind.

"He might be more handsome on the outside now, but he's gotten even weirder on the inside." Penelope tapped the screen. "Master's Revenge is the name of the game." She twisted her mouth to one side.

Elena glanced around conspiratorially. "Let's have a look around while he's gone."

The two women strolled across the wide decks and then made their way inside.

"This is a floating man cave," Elena said as they explored. "Big screens, casino gaming tables, bars on every level." She opened another door. "He even has a costume room."

Penelope looked over her shoulder at a room that had two makeup stations and racks of costumes. "Must have Halloween or masquerade parties on board."

"Or something..." Elena lifted an eyebrow.

They walked on and Elena came to an abrupt halt in front of a painting depicting a raging antihero with a voluptuous female victim cowering on the ground. "Ew. That's really disturbing. How can we get off this floating macho museum?"

Penelope paused outside an open door. Several large computer screens glowed in the dimly lit room. "Looks like his office." She started to turn around when something caught her eye. An image of her in New York floated on one screen, drawing her into the room.

She stepped inside.

A photograph of her from the New York event was on a tabloid website. A shiver coursed through her.

Elena followed her gaze. "He must really like you. Or he's stalking you."

The thought crossed her mind, but more likely he was concerned about her. Beneath the screen was a folder. Penelope took another step. Clipped to the top was a printed article with her photo. She reached out for it.

"The Jacuzzi isn't in here."

Penelope and Elena whirled around to face Kristo, who stood in the passageway behind them. He had a tight smile on his face.

"I just saw my photo as we were passing by."

Kristo held his arm out and motioned for them to come with him.

"Interesting art," Elena said, motioning toward the offensive painting as she stepped out.

"Don't like it?" Kristo frowned as he studied the artwork. "The designer chose it."

"It's misogynistic," Penelope said. "It depicts hatred and unnatural power over women."

"I can see how you'd find it offensive." Kristo held out his hand. "If you don't like it, I'll redecorate." His eyes glittered. "Or you can."

"Find a style *you* like." Penelope ignored his proffered hand and stepped from the room. After a moment, Elena hurried behind them.

As they walked through the luxurious vessel, Kristo relaxed and tucked his arm through Penelope's. "Until that nasty business in New York blows over, you could stay on board as long as you want. And I'll take you anywhere you want to go. No one can touch you here."

No one except him. Penelope glanced at his hand. From the way he squeezed her arm as he spoke, he was undoubtedly interested in more than her protection. "That's a kind offer, but I can take care of myself."

"I don't think you can. I saw photos of your home in the Hollywood Hills. You shouldn't have to deal with that mess. All those media trucks waiting for you to step outside your home. And a shooter on the loose. Why deal with that when I have the best security money can buy?"

Penelope shook her head. She didn't want to trade her protection for pair of velvet handcuffs...and who knew what else.

8

STEFAN RANG THE buzzer to the flat upstairs and waited. Early morning rays warmed the crisp autumn air. He'd flown directly to Copenhagen on an overnight flight. This wasn't his usual style—flying after a woman—but Penelope Plessen wasn't just any woman. He'd made a few mistakes in his life, and she was one of the largest ones. The other was Monica.

The intercom crackled. "Who is it?"

It was her. He cleared his throat. "Stefan."

The line went silent, and then popped again. "What?"

"It's Stefan Armstrong."

Penelope's voice sputtered through the line. "What are you doing here?"

He leaned in. "We need to talk—"

"I asked you not to contact me."

"It's important."

Silence.

"Second floor." The intercom buzzed.

Stefan breathed a sigh of relief and opened the door. He bounded up the interior stairs two at a time. When he reached the flat, the door swung open.

"I know you've come a long way," Penelope said, sounding guarded. "What's going on?"

Penelope always got right to the point, and he liked that. She stood in the doorway, barefoot and dressed in a white t-shirt and cut-off denim shorts that showed off her lean, muscular legs. Her hair was knotted at the nape of her neck. Without the makeup and clothes, he thought she was even more beautiful than in her photographs. Not that those weren't amazing, but as she stood before him, she nearly took his breath away, so intense was her fortitude and charisma. With her chin set like an Amazonian warrior, she stared at him with glowing tawny eyes, unblinking, waiting. He cleared his throat to speak.

"I've uncovered information you should know about." He put his hands on his hips. After the event in New York, he'd taken it upon himself to investigate. He looked around. "Is there somewhere else we can talk?"

"What's wrong with this place?"

"Outside is better."

She arched an eyebrow but slipped on a pair of sandals, pulled on a baseball cap and sunglasses, and then tapped on a closed door. "Elena, I'm going out for a walk. Sleep in and I'll see you later."

Stefan could hear a muffled reply, and then Penelope followed him out the door.

Fifteen minutes later, clutching steaming cups of coffee, they walked along a cobble-stoned road that lined the sea. The air seemed thinner and crisper here than in Los Angeles and the sun seemed slightly slanted at a different angle.

She listened intently while he explained why he'd come. "I did some investigating on the shooting," he said. Though he didn't want to alarm her, he did want to be straight with her. "One of my specialists in cyber surveillance has discovered some interesting things."

"Like what?"

"Some of the most egregious stories and photos of you are coming from sources that can't be easily tracked or located. Someone is hard at work planting stories about you. This is more Wiki-leaks than tabloid style."

"I see."

Penelope's voice was devoid of emotion and businesslike. He couldn't blame her after the grief he'd caused her. In doing what he thought was honorable, he'd destroyed his opportunity for the life he'd really wanted with her. He'd kicked himself many times for not deciding to take care of his child with Monica and be involved in his child's life, but continue seeing Penelope. They might've even been married.

But now, he had nothing. At least he could do right by Penelope this time. He drew his attention back to the reason he'd come.

Penelope was looking worried. "Who would be so interested in me?"

"That's what you need to find out." He glanced behind them. "I don't care if you use me or someone else, but in my professional opinion, you need close protective services right now. You need a bodyguard." He waited for her to laugh at him, the first nervous reaction many of his clients had.

But she didn't.

"Ever since I arrived, I've had an eerie feeling that I'm being watched, but I can't explain it."

"Listening to your gut is a good thing." In his experience, people often had feelings they couldn't explain that turned out to be valid. Maybe it was related to humankind's ancient fight-or-flight response, but Stefan always told people to listen to and trust their instinct. "But you need to do more than listen now. You need to take precautions."

"The detectives in New York haven't found anything about the shooter yet."

"They're always slammed. If you or other people had been hurt, more resources might've been channeled toward the crime."

"Next time, they might not miss." Penelope shook her head. "I've seen other women in my profession targeted and their lives and families destroyed." She heaved a labored sigh that Stefan knew was against her generally positive nature and added, "I need protection to prevent a future incident, that's what's you're saying. For how long?"

"Can't say, until the perpetrator is found, or the threat ceases." He stopped and turned to her, brushing a wisp of hair from her face. "I can provide any bodyguard you need, man or woman." He ached to hear her ask for his help, but he didn't want to be presumptuous. She'd nearly sent him away at her front door.

Penelope seemed to consider her options.

"They can follow me wherever I have to go for jobs?"

"Anywhere you want."

She stared out to sea, her eyes hidden behind oversized sunglasses. "I've been taking care of myself for years. But if anything happened to me—if I were shot and killed—it's my mom and dad who'd suffer. I'll do this for them, to spare them the agony."

"Where are they by the way?"

"They're spending two weeks at a spa in Thailand. I sent them there for their anniversary." She raked her teeth over her lower lip in thought. "A female bodyguard might be less obtrusive."

Stefan's heart sank. "No problem. I have a woman who's one of my very best bodyguards. I'll send her right over."

"This will change the way I live," she said, glancing at him. "Think it could blow over by itself?"

"Maybe. Maybe not. But that guy needs to be off the street. Do you remember Gianni Versace?"

She winced. "Everyone in fashion remembers his murder."

"John Lennon, Selena, Sharon Tate." He watched her reaction. "Shall I go on?"

A pained expression shadowed her face. "Okay, okay, I get it."

She pursed her perfect lips and Stefan could feel the ache in his gut. "I'll draw up an agreement that you and your attorney can review."

Stefan thought he understood what was going through her mind. When first signed, his clients often went through a range of emotions. The CEOs he worked for were generally accomplished, powerful people who had strong traits of self-reliance.

His company provided protective services to spouses and children, particularly in countries where kidnaping for ransom was frequent.

His celebrity clientele was different. Though accomplished, they were often young and inexperienced. Sudden fame and overnight success were hard to handle. They went from being an anonymous face to being recognized wherever they went.

Celebrities attracted stalkers like sticker burrs, and these dangerous super fans were as hard to get rid of, too. Even restraining orders didn't deter the most ardent, emotionally unbalanced fanatics. And that's where Penelope was now, grappling with someone who might want to claim notoriety through her murder and possibly others.

Stefan watched Penelope adjust her sunglasses against the morning rays. "Can we start when I return to L.A. next week?"

"Penelope, I have to recommend that we start now. The guy could follow you anywhere."

"But probably not outside of the U.S., right? Who would use a passport to follow someone they wanted to kill? That would leave a clear trail."

"These are psychopaths, they don't think like you do. They lack empathy and think they can't be touched. They want to possess the object of their desire. Or they don't care if they're caught. They might commit suicide afterward, or maybe they want the exposure. The point is, they're emotionally sick, Penelope. You can't apply normal reason to them."

"Okay, but I need to get used to this idea." Her phone buzzed and she pulled it out of her shorts pocket. Frowning, she scrolled through a text message.

"Everything okay?"

"Aside from a dozen messages from Kristo, my print job here was just cancelled. Guess the editor hadn't been keeping up with the latest news. My agent said the editor didn't want to be accused of jumping on the bandwagon of sensationalism." She tore off her sunglasses, angrily swiped her eyes with the back of her hand, and shoved them back on. "All my fashion shows have been cancelled, too."

"I'm not surprised." He paused. "Who's Kristo?"

She shrugged. "Just a friend I've known a while." She slipped the phone back into her pocket. "I'm effectively out of work, Stefan, so I have to create a new career. I have some ideas, but that's all. Security is going to be expensive, so unless I start getting paid again soon, my savings will be depleted fast."

It took all of his will power not to wrap his arms around her. Instead, he said, "Don't worry about the money. I owe you this one, Penelope. That's the least I can do."

She turned back toward the flat, hesitating. "Will you stay and go back to L.A. with me?"

Relief flooded him. "Sure. Whenever you want."

She turned and gave him a smile, one that had graced many magazine covers, but more than that, one that lit the fire in his heart.

9

"ABSOLUTELY NOT." STEFAN crossed his arms.

"I promised Elena I would take her to Tivoli Gardens," Penelope said. "I want to show her the places I loved as a child."

Where she'd always felt safe and happy, she thought, but didn't say it. They had only been back at the flat for half an hour, and already she was beginning to have second thoughts about this new professional arrangement with Stefan. "What's the problem?"

"Awful lot of people there."

"And none of them expect me to be there." She folded her arms across her chest, mimicking his stubborn behavior. She looked out the window to a quiet, flower box-lined, cobblestoned street below. A few people walked and others rode bikes, but everyone seemed to be minding their own business.

Now that Stefan was here, she didn't feel as anxious as she had been about her safety. Only about her attraction to him, despite their past. "I'll wear a hoodie." She picked up a red hooded sweatshirt that had been part of a designer's athletic collection she'd modeled.

"You're missing the point."

"No, you are. I have a life to live." She gestured at the magazines stacked around her. "This incident decimated my runway career, and it's trashing my commercial print work. At least give me a day of fun before I head back to L.A., because we both know what's waiting for me there."

Stefan shook his head. "You have to let me do my job."

"And I will. But nothing has happened here. You can start guarding when we return to the States." She narrowed her eyes at him. "I'm serious about this."

"So am I."

"Then you're fired." She picked up the hoodie. Maybe it was better this way.

"Better fired than seeing you dead." Stefan threw up his hands. "And for God's sake, don't wear that blazing red beacon. It's bad enough that your purple hair is an attractor. Don't you have anything in gray or brown?"

Elena dangled a gray hooded sweatshirt with the word Monterey stitched across the front. "I grabbed this on a chilly day on the peninsula. Will this do?"

Stefan grabbed it. "At least you understand."

Penelope snatched it from him. "Jeez, I can't believe both of you. You do realize that with my height I stand out anyway." She held up a strand of hair. "And then there's this."

"He's got a point," Elena said. "I have a whole wardrobe of black t-shirts and turtlenecks if you need it."

"Morbid. I've been trying to get you into colors forever."

Elena laughed. "Black shows off my jewelry well." She tossed

Stefan a black baseball cap. "Come with us."

Stefan caught the hat.

Penelope shrugged. "I guess if you want…" She darted a warning look at Elena. She loved her but wished she'd stop accepting or extending invitations without asking her.

As if she could read her mind, Elena winked at Penelope and mouthed the words, *but he's so handsome.*

Shaking her head, Penelope plunged her arms into the gray hoodie. "Let's go."

Stefan pulled on the cap. "Now that you mention it, can we do something about your hair?"

Both women turned to him at once and Penelope said, "No."

Elena grinned. "Wait a week or two."

Inside the gates of Tivoli, which was situated in the middle of Denmark, the amusement park was everything Penelope had remembered. They ate at the Biergarten, rode the old wooden rollercoaster that still had a brakesman driver on board, and listened to a symphony orchestra. Strolling around, they walked through flower gardens and past pretty lakes, and stopped to watch pantomimes at an outdoor theater.

Penelope showed them charming architecture that had been copied from China, India, and other countries around the world. "Even Walt Disney came here for inspiration for Disneyland," she told them, proud of her country.

After another ride, Penelope promised them a special indulgence. Now she stood with Elena and Stefan in line at Vaffelbageriet, a century-old ice cream shop, watching families with children laughing and playing. Idly she wondered if she would ever have the chance to bring children of her own here someday. She still had time, but she hadn't had a stellar relationship track record.

When their turn came, she stepped up and ordered ice cream scoops in waffle cones topped with whipped cream and a chocolate-covered meringue puff. "Here you are," she said, passing cones to Elena and Stefan. "This is some of the best ice cream in the world."

Elena laughed. "Where do you put all these calories? I'll be working out for days by the time I return to L.A."

"And you think I won't? I was blessed with a great metabolism, but I have to work out to stay fit, too. Otherwise I'd be living on lettuce like some of the models do. I'd rather be strong and fit than weak and skinny." Penelope noticed Stefan eyeing her, despite his best efforts not to. Jabbing him in the ribs, she was surprised at his still solid frame. "You're looking good. I'm impressed, rock solid abs."

"Working out more now," he said, coloring slightly. "Comes with the job description." He took a bite of his cone. "Now that's worth it," he said, a trace of a smile crossing his face.

"Glad to see you're finally loosening up," Penelope said.

"No, I'm not. I don't lose focus on the job." Quickly reverting, he wiped his mouth with a napkin.

"I fired you, remember?" Penelope scowled at him. "I'm not going to hire you again until we touch down in L.A."

Stefan shot her a look of concern. "I have a lot of arrangements to make. Like transportation to your house, which my team tells me is still under media siege. We'll probably need to upgrade your security, too."

"Enough," Elena said, cutting in. "I can't enjoy ice cream listening to you two."

"See, all that can wait," Penelope said, deliberately turning from Stefan. She knew all too well what awaited her at home. And this was her last day to enjoy herself for a while.

Penelope closed her eyes and licked her cone, memories of days spent here with her parents and grandparents calming her. She'd needed this visit, a touchstone of normalcy in a life that had become too hectic of late. Yet there wasn't much time to rest or reflect, because she had to return to work as quickly as possible. *If* she got work. The ice cream seemed to freeze a spot in her head and she winced.

"Brain freeze?" Elena giggled, shifting her eyes between Penelope and Stefan.

Penelope grinned and tapped her head until the delicious pain was gone. Of all of them, Elena was clearly having the best time.

After finishing their ice cream, they listened to music and stayed until the sun set. They were on their way out of the garden when a shooting, popping noise suddenly burst out.

Penelope's heart thumped and she ducked her head. "Wha—"

Stefan instinctively shielded Penelope against the side of a shop and whirled around, his eyes darting around the crowd.

"Oh, fireworks," Elena cried, clapping her hands and craning her neck to the darkened sky, which was illuminated with brilliant fiery designs.

Laughing with relief, Penelope slid down the wall to rest on her heels. "I can't believe we both fell for that. Fireworks!"

Stefan turned and grimaced. "Better to be safe."

"You have to admit that was funny," Penelope said, dabbing tears of laughter from her eyes. The release of pressure that had been building for days felt so good, she couldn't stop chuckling.

"Wow, Stefan's fast," Elena said, her eyes wide.

"You saw him in action in New York," Penelope said, rocking on her heels. The crowd around them started laughing, too, yet Stefan remained on high alert, his body tense and his eyes taking in everything around them.

"Get up," he said, holding his hands to her while he glanced around.

Penelope tentatively threaded her hands with his, recalling his touch on the balcony of his apartment in New York. She closed her eyes, missing the warmth of his large, capable hands entwined with her slender fingers. This small movement wrenched lose feelings she'd bottled up inside, and a deep yearning for all that could have been—no, *should* have been—between them rushed into the core of her being, leaving her weak with regret.

Her laughter subsided, and she tossed her hair to one side, obscuring tears that spilled relentlessly forth.

"Hey, hey," Stefan said, turning his attention to her and lifting her to her feet. "You're shaking."

She let him think it was because she'd been frightened. For a moment, she'd let her guard down around him, but she couldn't risk it again. Still, his touch, his hands wrapped around her arms, cradling her shoulders—it was almost more than she could bear.

"You're safe now," he whispered to her. "I understand."

Did he? What was it he thought he understood? She wondered if he knew how difficult it was to keep a heart from breaking. He enfolded her in his arms and she rested against him, wishing that their lives had worked out differently, yet unable to risk the chance of devastation again.

10

THE NEXT MORNING, Elena peeked through the shutters, which were closed at Stefan's request. "Are you sure the photographers out there didn't come with Stefan? They weren't there yesterday."

"Neither were those pictures that were posted online." Penelope shoved a pair of running shoes she'd bought at an airport boutique into her suitcase. Their idyllic visit had come to an abrupt end when shots of her and Elena shopping in Illum, a popular department store, and riding the roller coaster at Tivoli were posted online and members of the press began ringing the apartment at six a.m. As soon as she'd awakened she'd seen the images, which sent chills through her.

She could only imagine that regular people must have posted photos from their phones, which in turn tipped off the tabloids. Grabbing loose clothing from the bed, she stuffed it hastily into the open case, angry over the invasion of privacy.

In the past, she'd always handled recognition graciously, though she'd never felt stalked or cornered before. Copenhagen had always been her refuge. She wondered if there was any place she'd ever feel safe again. "Are you ready?"

"Almost." Elena flipped the shutter louvers closed.

Stefan waited at a table near the front door. He'd set up his computer and was speaking to his team in California. Penelope could hear him arranging the transportation from the airport to her home, and she was relieved that he was managing this task. The last time she'd tried to go home, she couldn't even get near it.

Stefan leaned back in his chair. "We need to get to the airport soon."

Penelope snapped her suitcase shut. "I'm ready."

Once they were outside, Stefan guided them through the media that was camped outside the door to her apartment and cleared the path to the airport.

As they drove, Stefan checked his phone. "Did you know that another threat has been received?"

Penelope turned in her seat in the car and stared at him. "A threat? Where?"

"It was mailed to your home."

"I don't understand, who received it?" Penelope was trying to make sense of what was happening, but she had a lot on her mind. Her housekeeper was away, too. She would have normally checked the mail.

"Evidently someone got to your mailbox and opened the mail."

Penelope was horrified. "But I have a locking mailbox."

"Wait a minute." Elena spoke up in the backseat. "Isn't that a federal offense?"

Stefan grinned grimly in the rearview mirror of the black sedan. "Sure, but who's going to prosecute? Tabloid reporters will risk it to get the story."

Once they were safely ensconced on the plane, Penelope slipped on headphones and watched movies, though she was unable to relax. The pressure she felt building from canceled jobs was weighing on her mind, and she had to come up with another career plan fast.

She glanced to her side where Elena slept soundly. Across the aisle sat Stefan, who'd remained on relaxed alert throughout the long flight. Penelope wondered how he did it.

Penelope began to pencil out ideas while she formulated a new plan for her future. By the time the flight attendants were serving breakfast and Elena woke up, Penelope had come up with several ideas she thought might be viable.

"Elena, would you be open to producing a private label jewelry line?"

"Depends." Elena said, sipping her coffee. "Are you talking about a line with your name on it?"

"That's right. It's one of the ideas that I've been thinking about."

"Where would you want to sell it?"

"Possibly a shopping network. I'd like to pitch it as a collaboration with you."

Elena shook her head. "I appreciate that, but with your name you would probably be better off pitching it as your own line, though I can handle the production." Her brown eyes flashed as she thought about it."

Penelope stretched in her seat.

"What else do you have in mind?" Elena pinched off a piece of a warm croissant.

"Possibly something for television."

Elena jerked her head up. "You mean, like a reality show?"

"No way. I've given up enough privacy. Maybe a contest for new models. I could involve Fianna and have some of her designs showcased on the show."

"That would be interesting." Elena appeared thoughtful. "You've mentioned diversification in the past. You think it's time now?"

"At the rate my cancellations are going, I could easily lose the rest of the year. Or more. Once designers and companies start replacing you, it's hard to get back into the game. I've seen it happen to others."

Elena nodded thoughtfully. "Have you thought of working with Fianna on a fashion line?"

"I have. And I'm already working with Dahlia on a fragrance and with Olga Kaminsky on a High Gloss color line." Frowning, she made a note to talk to Dahlia about the fragrances she'd created for her. The negative media attention could have adverse effects, and she wanted to warn her about her production quantity.

"Sounds like you're pretty busy already."

"I need to get serious about it now and figure out how to increase volume." What she was concerned about, but didn't say, was that Olga could discontinue the line if the negative press began to affect sales. She would also try to limit exposure in some way for Elena. "I have a lot more to learn about entrepreneurship."

"I'll help you as much as I can," Elena said. "It was a struggle to make the first few sales. Then, it was a battle to produce enough inventory. Now, I'm concerned about the turnover of the inventory, and taking the line to a higher artistic level."

Penelope nodded, listening. "That's a lot to consider."

"And I've done it all on a shoestring budget. Now I'm at the point where I have to consider growth and distribution. For example, do I continue to sell exclusively in my store, or do I begin to sell into department stores?"

"Why wouldn't you sell to department stores?"

"There's plenty to think about, such as lower margins, increased advertising and sales support, higher inventory costs, and less control over sales." Elena laughed. "And that's just the beginning."

"Then there's a lot to think about before we start talking about designs."

"That's the part I love most. It's why I do what I do. I feel like there's this wellspring of creativity that comes bubbling out of me and I have to serve it in order to feel complete as an artist. Does that make sense?"

Penelope had observed this in her other friends, from Verena to Fianna to Dahlia. Each of them envisioned and created things they loved—skincare, fashion, and perfume. They put their own unmistakable stamp on their creations. It was the authenticity, excellence, and point of view that attracted women to their products.

Could she do the same? From working with designers, she knew success often came down to branding, so it was up to her to determine what her personal brand would be. That was the vision she needed to develop first, and then she could decide where to go with it.

Penelope stirred her coffee. "You've been a great help, Elena. You've given me a lot to think about before I take the plunge."

She sipped her coffee and eased back in her seat. From the corner of her eye, she could see Stefan watching her. He'd been listening to her conversation with Elena, yet he showed no sign of interest. *Is this the way it's going to be between us?* Then she remembered that Stefan was arranging a female bodyguard to work with her in Los Angeles. With a jolt, she realized she would miss him.

Then she wondered what it would take for him to stay.

11

Hollywood Hills, California

STEFAN GUIDED PENELOPE and Elena through the secured area of the Los Angeles airport. The SUV he'd arranged was idling by the curb at LAX. He scanned the area, spying a couple of photographers with long lens cameras, but he saw no one who looked like they might want to cause Penelope harm. As long as they kept their distance, they could take photos, but his job was to ensure her safety.

"This way, ladies," he said, as one of his employees, Josh, led them to the SUV.

Leaning toward him and touching his arm, Penelope paused. "You have no idea how much I appreciate this."

Her hand rested a little too long on his arm, but he made no movement. "I'll have one of our female bodyguards take over as soon as I have one available," he replied, maintaining his composure. He wanted to assign the best person they had for her. Penelope smiled with gratitude, and he returned a curt nod. *Focus,* he reminded himself, dropping back.

Walking behind Penelope, Stefan had a hard time keeping his eyes from following her well-proportioned frame under her slim white shirt and blue jeans. He'd told her to dress in a manner that wouldn't attract attention, but it hardly mattered. Anything she wore would attract attention.

Why anyone would want to hurt her was beyond him, but he'd learned long ago that there were truly disturbed people in the world who considered reasonable thought an inconvenient shackle. Such as the man who'd taken a shot at Penelope.

Stefan tore his eyes away from her long, lean legs, chastising himself. He had a job to do and personal involvement would only mar his judgement. In critical split seconds, the correct rapid decisions could mean the difference between life and death.

Once inside the SUV, Stefan sat in the front while Josh steered from the airport. A highly trained former New York policeman, Josh had taken early retirement to be closer to his parents, who had retired in Palm Springs. Few could match his diligence.

Their work at the airport hadn't been complicated, but as soon as they approached Penelope's street in Hollywood Hills, he knew they were in for difficulties. Looking up the hill from Hollywood Boulevard, he spied media trucks with communication equipment poking through the trees.

"Trouble ahead," he said to Josh. Turning to Penelope and Elena in the backseat, he added, "You may want to get down. The windows are darkened, but people can see through the windshield."

Penelope tilted her chin. "I refuse to hide from photographers on my way home."

"Look, I admire your courage, but Josh and I are here to protect you against a very real threat, not tabloid photographers."

Penelope shot him a withering look.

At the end of their ascent from Hollywood Boulevard, Josh attempted to steer the SUV into a sharp left turn at the top of the hill, but a media truck blocked the narrow street to all but the smallest cars. With measured deliberateness, he executed a crisp three-point turn and edged past the truck, rolling over a curb on the other side.

Glancing behind him, Stefan could see Penelope and Elena holding their breath as the SUV squeezed past. The side mirrors were a feather's breath away from the media truck.

Elena gasped and ducked down.

"Watch out," Penelope yelled, leaning forward into the back of Stefan's seat.

A man leaped in front of their SUV with a shoulder-held video camera, running backwards while filming them as they wove through an obstacle course of oversized garbage containers, neighbors' cars, and media vans parked on either side of the narrow street. Two more photographers ran along beside them, and Stefan spotted another paparazzi wedged in a tree.

"Ever been like this before?" Stefan asked. As the verbal alarm for Penelope's arrival rang through the crowd, others gathered perilously close to the vehicle.

"It's usually pretty quiet up here," Penelope said, biting her lip. "Several actors and singers live up here for that reason." She drew back from the window. "I'll sure hear about this from them."

"Hang on," Stefan replied, gritting his teeth as Josh steered through them at an excruciatingly slow pace. "Get down, both of you," he repeated, looking back at Penelope and Elena. "See that guy in the tree there?

"That's just a photographer," Penelope said.

"Is it?" he shot back. "Think a guy crazy enough to climb a tree might also have a gun?"

Elena ducked, while Penelope slithered down with an insolent look on her face.

Stefan turned back. He didn't care what Penelope thought; he was doing what was required to keep her out of harm's way.

Josh flashed his headlights and proceeded with cautious determination. When they finally reached her house, Stefan got out to open the garage using the code Penelope had given him and Josh pulled in next to Penelope's pearly white Tesla.

Penelope started to open the rear door.

"Wait until the garage door closes and I give you the signal before getting out of the car." Stefan got out and checked the garage. Satisfied that no one was waiting for them, he opened her door.

Penelope hesitated, then got out. Was she waiting for him to help her as he'd once done when they dated, or was she finally grasping the severity of the situation? The last thing he needed right now was for her to get an attitude.

Sometimes clients called his company, desperate for help, and then, once they felt safer, unconsciously fed a psychological need for control by going to great lengths to show how much they didn't need the services of his firm.

Penelope stepped from the car.

"You need to change the code on your garage door," he told her.

"Why?"

"Anyone can look up your birthday online. Is it the same on your front door?"

Penelope stepped past him. "When is your female guard coming over?"

"As soon as possible."

She marched to the door that led into the Spanish-styled house, its arches framed with lush pink bougainvillea. Splashes of pink and white geraniums and purple daisies spilled from terra cotta pots placed along the driveway. Hand-painted tiles lined the curved entry door.

Stefan put a hand on her shoulder. "Wait just a minute." He stepped in front of her. "No security system?"

"This house was originally built in the 1950s. I've been meaning to put one in."

He tried the door to the house. It opened under his hand. "You need to keep this door locked." They'd only been there a couple of minutes and already he could tell that her security was full of holes.

"It usually is," she replied in an icy tone. She glanced at a note the woman had left for her on a table in the foyer. "My housekeeper must have accidently left it open."

He frowned. "You didn't say you had a housekeeper."

Penelope rolled her eyes. "Just tell me everything your other bodyguard will need to know before she gets here."

Stefan indicated a wooden bench in the foyer. "Stay here while I check the house."

Penelope plopped down on it, tapping her heel on the Saltillo-tiled floor.

As he stepped down into the living room, the heady scent of flowers filled the air. Bouquets of white lilies, tuberose, and roses were placed on the entry table, coffee table, side tables, and mantle. "Looks like a florist shop," he muttered to himself.

He spotted a stack of florist's cards under one bouquet, picked them up, flipped through them, and then slid them into his pocket. They were all from one man. In his experience, this wasn't normal behavior.

While Josh helped Elena with luggage, Stefan began to take inventory of the house. To one side, glass windows looked out over a steep hillside covered in vegetation. Ivy, bougainvillea, and lantana crept across the slope, anchoring the topsoil. On the other side, a deck wrapped around the west side of the house, with deck chairs angled toward a long pool. He remembered how much Penelope liked to swim and made a note to secure the area as much as possible and to alert the new bodyguard. He checked a door. At least it was locked.

All at once, he heard a scream from a hallway behind him. He raced toward it, slamming through a doorway.

"Get out of here!" Wearing only a lacy bra and her jeans, Penelope was brandishing a wooden baseball bat. Her white shirt was on the bed where she had probably been changing. A man was scaling the rear railing to her patio, a camera jerking around his neck as he leaped over the fence, hitting the massive bougainvillea bush that trailed over it, releasing a shower of purple flowers. Racing to the sliding glass door, she thrust open the door, bat in hand.

At the top of the railing, he turned and snapped his camera, then fell backward from the patio.

"You're trespassing," she yelled, taking a step outside.

She didn't get far. "Don't go after him!" Stefan hurtled toward her and caught the back of her jeans, causing her to fall back inside the bedroom. Tumbling to the floor, Stefan tugged the bat from her and tossed it onto the enormous bed behind them. "Nice grip, but what the hell do you think you're doing?"

"Let me go, he's getting away," she yelled, struggling against him.

Stefan rolled on top of her and pinned her to a patterned rug covering the floor. She was wearing a beige-colored lace bra that had little sparkles of gold thread running—*stop it.* He dragged his attention back to her eyes, which were flashing with fury. Through the open door, he could hear a scuffle beyond the patio. Recognizing Josh's grunts, he figured his partner had apprehended the perpetrator.

In exasperation, Penelope tried to blow strands of hair stuck in her glossy lips. "You should be going after him."

"Josh's got him." He plucked the hair from her full mouth, trying not to let his gaze linger there. "You should have better security."

She made a face. "I never needed it before. This is a quiet

117

neighborhood."

"The neighborhood has changed." After releasing her, he helped her up from the floor and then tossed her discarded shirt to her. He turned away from her while she put it on.

It took everything in him not to fold her into his arms and smother her face with kisses. Performing protective services was all in a day's work to him, but based on his feelings for her, he also felt the need to comfort her. And that was strictly out of line. She'd made it clear to him after dinner in New York that she wanted nothing to do with him. That was fine with him, he told himself; he'd have his best woman on the job within a day or two. He blew out a breath. "Decent yet?"

"Don't you have to go help Josh?"

Turning around, Stefan grinned. "Josh is doing fine. I doubt you'll see that photographer around here again."

Glancing around the bedroom, he noticed more flowers. "Nice flowers," he said, and tossed the cards onto a nightstand.

Penelope snatched them up and read a couple of them.

"We'll need to talk to him." Stefan tamped down uncharacteristic tension that rose within him.

"Kristo's not the problem. He's not even in L.A."

She stared at him, but he was unable to read her level expression. *Kristo again. Who the hell is he?* His gut twisted into coils.

"Why did I ever let you talk me into doing this?" she asked, still staring at him.

"Because you trust me." He picked up the baseball bat.

Elena appeared at the door to the bedroom out of breath, her eyes wide. "What happened? I heard you scream." Her mouth dropped open as she took in the scene with Penelope buttoning her shirt and Stefan holding a baseball bat. "Uh, did I interrupt something?"

Penelope let out a nervous laugh. "There was a photographer outside, and I was going after him." She put a hand on her hip. "I succeeded in scaring him off."

Stefan handed her the bat. "Here you go, slugger, though you won't need this as long as I'm around."

"It's a memento." She hefted the bat. "I was in a celebrity baseball game for a charity this summer."

Elena raced to Penelope and gave her a hug. "I never realized how frightening being a celebrity could be. And I thought you had to have nerves of steel to walk the runway. That's nothing compared to what you go through off stage."

"It's starting to look like this is all part of the job, isn't it?" Penelope glanced down at her hands. "Got to wash off the airport grime." She walked into the adjoining dressing area into the bathroom.

A split second later, she screamed.

12

PENELOPE STOOD ROOTED in her bathroom, shocked at the enlarged magazine cover photo plastered to the mirror above her wide makeup vanity. Bullet holes marked the center of her forehead, neck, and heart, while blood dripped down her face and throat, splashing onto her chest. It was the most gruesome image of herself she'd ever seen. It was so graphic, she covered her face with her hands and whirled away from it.

At the sound of her scream, Stefan rushed in and wrapped his arms around her, guiding her away from the abhorrent photo. "Stay in the bedroom with Elena and let me check this out," he said, urgency evident in his voice. As she stepped out, she heard him radio his partner Josh.

This time she did as he instructed while he searched her dressing area, bathroom, and closet. Someone had actually been in her home, in her private domain, and this unnerved her. This was the sort of thing that happened to other big stars, not to her. Even though her photos were found on every newsstand and website, she'd always managed to live quietly in the Hollywood Hills.

She clutched Elena, who was peeking over her shoulder.

"Oh no," Elena said, her eyes widening when she saw the image. "This is bad. Do you have any idea who might've done this?"

Too stunned to talk, Penelope could only shake her head. She set her jaw and gritted her teeth in an attempt to maintain control.

Shortly, Stefan appeared in the entryway to the bedroom. "Where was that photo taken?"

"I've never shot a photo like that. It's been altered from a *Fashion News Daily* magazine cover."

"Those are actual bullet holes." Stefan paced the bedroom, searching for clues. "We need to call the police on this one. That's evidence, and they may be able to glean something to find out who's behind it." He stopped and squatted, pointing to part of a muddy bit on the floor. "Don't disturb that."

"It's got to be the same man from New York," Elena said.

"Not necessarily," Stefan said, standing. "Don't touch anything in here." He pulled his phone from his pocket.

Penelope felt a chill come over her like nothing she'd ever experienced before. A stranger had infiltrated her home, violating her private sanctuary. A shiver seized her and she fought the feeling, trying to remain calm. She told herself to breathe, but she found herself choking up.

She heard Josh outside the house, but couldn't make out what was going on. Stefan locked the exterior door and guided her and Elena from the scene in the bedroom.

"Wait here," Stefan said, his voice stern. "This time, don't go wandering off."

Even though Stefan was doing his job, she wished she could go wherever she liked. This was her home, and being captive was not part of her plan. After seeing that photo, all she wanted was to get away from her home again. But where could she go that she wouldn't be found?

Her plan was to get rid of Stefan as soon as she could. His presence was disturbing and distracting. Just minutes ago when he'd straddled her in the bedroom to keep her from chasing the photographer, she'd had an overwhelming urge to throw her arms around him and caress the lips she recalled as being the most tender, sensual lips she'd ever kissed. She ran a hand over her messy hair, trying to squelch the warm sensation that insisted on growing deep within her.

She needed to find work as soon as possible and that infuriatingly handsome man was a disruption she couldn't afford for long. His company should be charging a precious daily rate so that he could continue to protect—and annoy—her. Although he'd indicated otherwise, she would certainly ask for a bill. She didn't want to owe him a thing.

Elena stared after Stefan. "He still really cares for you."

Penelope gave a shaky laugh. "Can't depend on him, though." She recalled the day he'd told her he had slept with Monica. She'd been so hurt, and since then, she'd vowed that she would never let a man do that to her again. Especially not Stefan.

"Seems pretty dependable to me," Elena said. "I've never had a boyfriend look out for me the way he does for you."

"That's just business. Don't confuse his need to excel on the job with actual concern." Still shaking with shock, Penelope perched on the steps that led from the entry down to the living area.

From where she sat, she could see from Santa Monica on the west to downtown Los Angeles on the east. She breathed in, focusing on the distant horizon. This view was usually calming, but today her mind was consumed by Stefan's increasingly irritating presence.

Outside, the sound of sirens cut through the usual sound of street traffic rising from Fairfax Avenue. Lights flashed through the traffic.

Elena plopped next to her. "I've never heard you speak like this. Do you still care for him?"

Penelope shrugged. The truth was, she had never completely banished him from her heart. He was the gold standard by which she measured all other men, and none had ever approached his worth.

Elena glanced nervously behind her. "I hope they don't find anything else in the house. Want me to stay over tonight?"

"I'd really like that." Penelope expelled a breath of relief and clasped Elena's hand. She'd been worried about Stefan staying over. He'd told her she would have someone with her around the clock, but she could handle just so much of Stefan.

The police sirens grew louder, followed by a loudspeaker. The police were directing the media vans from the street.

"Hey, you're shaking," Elena said, squeezing her hand. "You were looking pretty fierce when I walked in on you."

"I'm sure that was adrenaline." In actuality, she'd never used the bat before to defend herself. A solid jab, a swift kick—yes, but never a weapon of any sort. She just wanted to get rid of the guy.

"And that baseball bat…" Elena started laughing. "Wonder if the photographer got a shot of that?"

The sound of Elena's laughter broke through her distress and despite her worry, a little chuckle slipped out. "He caught me as I was changing clothes, so if he did, a shot of me wearing a bra and wielding a baseball bat like some deranged Amazonian warrior should be a hot post on social media tomorrow."

Elena burst out laughing, and Penelope joined in. They were so on edge that laughter came as a relief. Once they started, they couldn't stop, and soon the two women were clutching each other as tears of laughter wet their cheeks.

"Want the police to think this was a farce?" Stefan stood behind them frowning, his hands on his hips, surveying the scene.

Elena made a face, teasing him. "Give the woman a break, huh?"

Penelope could see that Stefan was in no mood to joke around. She appreciated what he was doing for her, but she'd reached the point where she needed to change her focus and unwind. "Relax, we'll behave," Penelope said, which sent Elena into another fit of laughter.

The police sirens ceased outside, and moments later a hard knock sounded on the door.

"Here we go again," Elena said, catching her breath. "At least I'm meeting a lot of cute police officers."

Penelope grinned, wiping tears of laughter from her eyes. "That's usually my line."

Stefan shot them a stern look as he opened the door.

After the police took their statements, photographed the interior and exterior, and took samples, they left Penelope's house. Sitting at the kitchen table with Elena in the aquamarine glass-tiled kitchen, she passed her hands across her face. "Thank goodness they're gone."

"And the paparazzi with them." Their vans were blocking the street, so on an order of the fire marshal, they were required to move.

"Want to bet they'll be back on foot?" Penelope grimaced, glancing around her house.

"So who are all the flowers from?" Elena asked, glancing around. "Don't tell me this is normal. Or did someone die?"

Penelope gave her a puzzled smile. "Kristo. My housekeeper must have taken the delivery." She wasn't sure how she felt about this overwhelming gesture.

"This is outrageous." Elena's eyes widened. "Beautiful, but way overboard."

Penelope nodded. "I've watched his transformation from geeky nerd to master of the universe. He can't always express himself—that's what I remember most about him. He used to stutter when he got around large groups of people, and took lessons to overcome it. Maybe this is his way of apologizing for that awful game photo of me."

"Or because he seemed awkward after he found us in his office." Elena angled her head toward the floral arrangements. "I like the way he apologizes. It's a great start," she added with a wink. "But you're right, he's still odd."

Penelope's phone buzzed, and she pulled it from her pocket. A message from her agent floated across the screen. Another cancellation. And more messages from Kristo. She put her phone down and spun it around.

Elena leaned over. "Who's that from?"

"My agent. I've got to put my life back together." Penelope knew it might never be the same, because once a model left the runway, she was easy to replace, but she had to figure out her next career move. She grinned at Elena. "How about getting out of here?"

"Where do you want to go?"

Penelope scanned her text messages. "My friend Eva is having a party tonight." She'd met the model through her friend Scarlett, who'd handle her licensing deal with Olga Kaminsky at High Gloss.

"Who's Eva?" Elena asked.

"Another model, and someone you should know. I met her through Scarlett, whose friend Jen is Eva's contract attorney. Eva is well-connected with Hollywood people."

Stefan walked in. "You're not going out to a party."

Penelope stood to face him. "It might look like a party to you, but I'm networking." She snapped her fingers in his face. "Let's roll."

13

"YOU CAN DROP us there at the side entrance," Penelope said, leaning toward Josh. They were cruising down Sunset Boulevard, which was jam packed on a Friday night. Neon lights flashed a rainbow of colors across the interior of the SUV, and music blasted from neighboring cars. Lines formed in front of popular clubs. Penelope ignored Stefan, who was sitting in the passenger seat in front of her and Elena.

"I'm going in, too." Stefan's jaw was set tight. He'd acquiesced, but he clearly wasn't happy about it. She'd reminded him that he wasn't there to run her life; he was only there to protect her.

Penelope opened her mouth to protest, but then thought better of it. If he hadn't been there when she'd arrived home, she would have been terrified at seeing the gruesome photograph in her bathroom. She shivered as she thought about it, but she was not going to let some nut job hinder her actions.

"Give me your purse," Stefan said.

"What?"

"Your purse."

She was wearing a small cross-body bag she'd recently picked up at a Tory Burch sample sale in New York during Fashion Week. "I will not."

Stefan gave her a look. "I have a security device I want to affix to it. If we get separated and you need help, you can reach me. It's discreet." He held up a tiny device.

She slipped the purse off and handed it to him, watching as he snapped a tiny device along the upper edge of the bag, and then he showed her how to activate it to connect to an earpiece he wore.

"That's pretty cool," Elena said, as Penelope tested it.

Grudgingly, Penelope had to agree. Though the thought that she might have to use it was still unsettling, it was more compact than a baseball bat. She smiled at Stefan. "Thanks."

Satisfied, he turned his attention back to the road ahead.

"I feel like I had my own personal stylist tonight," Elena said, admiring the slim Pucci dress that Penelope had chosen for her. "Thanks for the fashion therapy. I feel like I can conquer anything in this."

"I had to get you out of your black uniform." Penelope apprised her friend. She'd enjoyed putting together an outfit that would help her shine—and one she'd feel confident in. "That colorful print really sets off your jewelry."

To Penelope, fashion was akin to therapy. Her mother had suffered from poor self-image and lack of confidence. Penelope had helped her regain her sense of self by creating outfits that projected a positive new image. *I feel like I can do anything in this*, her mother would say.

"Some people scoff at fashion," Penelope said. "But clothing sends a powerful message, not the least of which is to the person wearing it. It's a phenomenon called enclothed cognition. As you dress, so you are."

Penelope knew that models and actors had long known the heightened value of transformation and presentation, but only recently had researchers confirmed the link in this phenomenon. While she was completing her degree at the University of Southern California in the evenings, she'd read the research in a psychology journal, intrigued that some people really could gain psychological strength from the clothing they wore.

"If your brain links success with an outfit, you're more likely to actually take on those attributes when you wear it," Penelope explained.

Josh spoke up. "That's like putting on a police uniform."

"Exactly." Penelope tapped his shoulder and smiled.

"I wonder about software designers who live in jeans and t-shirts," Josh said. "They're living in mansions in Silicon Valley, but you'd never know it by what they wear."

Elena chimed in. "They must be saying that their value is their brain, not their physical appearance."

Tonight, Penelope was channeling vintage Hollywood with glossy red lipstick, an off-the-shoulder, midriff-baring top, and wide-legged pants. She'd curled her hair into a sassy Marilyn Monroe style, and added a pair of Elena's bold amethyst earrings. She glanced down. Considering her outfit, she was mimicking the styles she'd loved on strong, smart, glamorous actresses like Doris Day and Ginger Rogers, women who took on Hollywood

129

to build careers and personal empires.

"Enough with the fashion therapy," Stefan said. "We're here."

The secret side entrance at the hotel led directly to the rooftop bar and pool where Eva Devereaux loved to throw parties.

A doorman at a nondescript entrance stopped them. "Sorry, private party tonight."

"We're on the list." Penelope gave her name and the doorman consulted his clipboard. "You're down for two." As he looked from Elena to Stefan, his smile faded. "Which one's coming with you?"

"Both."

"I'm sorry—"

Stefan stepped forward and flashed a card at the man. "I'm the bodyguard."

"Oh yeah, heard about all that crap in New York." The man quickly nodded and buzzed them up.

When they stepped off the elevator, Penelope took in the ivy-covered walls, potted palms, open air bar, and twinkling lights. A pool shimmered in the middle of the rooftop patio and the lights of Los Angles stretched out beyond them. Music thumped in the background and perfume wafted across the beautiful crowd.

Elena whirled around. "This place is amazing."

"Wait until you see who's here," Penelope said. Eva Devereaux was a top model who was the face of beauty giant Tilly Pop. She was also one of the few people who'd reached out to her after the incident. While the cancellations were mounting, Eva was encouraging her to get out and join her. With each passing day, Penelope was beginning to appreciate friends like that more and more.

A tall woman with wavy, strawberry blond hair spied them and waved.

"There she is," Penelope said, making her way through the crowd. She greeted Eva with a hug and introduced Elena.

"Penelope, I haven't seen you since the launch party for Catwalk Paradise," Eva said.

"Oh, I love that fragrance," Elena said.

"And I love your jewelry," Eva replied. Under finely shaped, expressive eyebrows, her blue-gray eyes widened. "I've never seen anything quite like it."

Elena beamed, showing off an earring. "It's mine. I design it."

Eva immediately hooked her arm with Elena's and said to Penelope, "You always bring the most interesting people to my parties. We're going to have a lot to talk about." She glanced behind Penelope. "And is this gorgeous man with you?"

Penelope stepped aside. "This is Stefan Armstrong. He's my..."

"Friend." Stefan smiled and shook her hand.

"Nice friends," Eva replied with a wink.

Two women, both in their thirties, joined them. Penelope exchanged hugs with Scarlett and her friend Jen, Eva's contract attorney.

"Scarlett, what a surprise seeing you here." Penelope introduced Elena and Stefan to Jen. She was surprised that Stefan was keeping a low profile and hadn't identified himself as a body-guard. Just as she was thinking that, he caught her eye. A smile played on his face that she couldn't read. Was he mocking her? She glanced away.

"Jen got me in," Scarlett said, grinning. "I've been in court all week on a trademark dispute, and I couldn't wait to shed my courtroom clothes tonight."

Turning serious, Eva said to Penelope, "How are you doing? And have they caught the guy yet?"

"The police are looking for him," Penelope said, keeping a calm expression, though she felt like screaming inside.

Seeming to pick up on Penelope's distress, Stefan put his arm around her. "Any leads you might have, no matter how small, would be appreciated."

Scarlett caught his comment right away. Looking over his broad, muscular physique, she asked, "Are you a police officer?"

"Bodyguard. And old friend." He gave her a reassuring little hug as he spoke.

Penelope smiled wanly at him, watching as her friend's mouths formed silent Os in polite response. Having a bodyguard wasn't unusual in Hollywood, but it was mostly top singers who had millions of young, wildly devoted and emotional fans, or an actress who'd acquired a stalker. She tried not to think about Stefan's arm around her. She shivered—only because it was a lit-tle cool outside here on the roof, she told herself.

Eva continued. "I've heard a lot of designers have cancelled your contracts."

"You shouldn't be financially harmed for this," Jen said.

"Have Scarlett look at your contracts."

Scarlett nodded. "Although that incident was something out of your control, the designers have a duty to protect their other models and patrons, too. Still, there might be liquidated damages clauses. You could collect something." She pressed Penelope's hand as she spoke. "Call me tomorrow. You shouldn't be black-listed."

Penelope sucked in a breath. *Blacklisted.* The word sliced through her confidence. "I just want to work again," Penelope said, hating the helpless feeling encroaching upon her.

With one act, that disturbed man had put her in this position. She had a strong work ethic, and she felt stymied by not being able to fill her calendar as she had for years. Straightening her shoulders, she said, "I have a new idea, and I'm looking for television executives who might be interested."

Eva ran her thumb along her chin in thought. "You should talk to Lele Rose, she's been in L.A. a long time. She's worked with costume designers at the studios. They use her L.R. brand a lot. She may know of someone." She swiveled in her shimmering pink dress, scanning the crowd. "I saw her here earlier."

"I know who she is." Penelope gazed across the deck. "I'll look for her." To Scarlett she added, "Go and circulate. This party is full of people who could use your services."

"I've got to run, too," Eva said. "The Tilly Pop president just arrived and I have to say hello."

As Scarlett, Jen, and Eva moved on, Elena turned to Penelope. "Television, that's intriguing."

Penelope twisted her lips to one side. "I figure they can't

shoot me on a closed set."

"Not bad thinking," Stefan said, letting his arm slide off of her.

"Glad you approve." She'd been thinking of opportunities where her sudden notoriety could actually be an asset.

"Look at the Kardashians and all the other reality show stars," Elena said. "The more controversy in their lives, the higher their ratings."

"I'm still forming ideas. Something to do with beauty, fashion, and positive self-image." Penelope knew that controversial topics were hot among the networks and cable channels, but she wanted to make positive contributions. *Would that sell?* She wondered.

A waiter stopped by with a tray of champagne, and Penelope and Elena each took a flute. Stefan waved it off, as Penelope knew he would. After all, he was on duty.

As she sipped her champagne, she watched Stefan from the corner of her eye. He was scrutinizing everyone at the party, and had positioned himself by her side so that he could protect her.

She relaxed a little, knowing that he was there for her, but the intense attraction of his physical presence was still unnerving. Why couldn't she get over this man? Just when she thought that she'd made up her mind, her body betrayed her. Every time he was near her, she had physical sensations over which she had little control.

Irritated by this thought, Penelope turned toward the crowd. "There's Lele," she said, nodding toward a woman who could be anywhere between forty and sixty years old with an obvious wig of straight shimmering red hair and an armful of bangles. She'd met her through Betsey Johnson, the designer known for whimsical styles and for doing cartwheels down the runway at the end of her fashion shows.

Elena nudged her and said, "You need to talk to her."

"I will. I did some work for her a while back." Penelope wedged her way through the crowd, which began to open for her once people recognized her. She'd had a lot more airplay in the tabloids and on social media than ever before. But that didn't pay the bills.

Elena leaned toward her, gushing with enthusiasm. "Isn't that Hugo Gutierrez over there? He's so hot in that TV show, *Creatures of Slaughter Creek.* Oh, he's talking to—oh God, what's his name?"

Penelope smiled at the excitement dancing in her friend's eyes. "It's Elijah Rousseau. Rumor has it he just landed a role on the show with Hugo."

"I think I'm going to faint." Elena waved her hand on her flushed face theatrically.

Stefan arched an eyebrow at her. "Want me to introduce you to Hugo?"

"You *know* Hugo Gutierrez?"

Penelope laughed. Elena loved binge watching television shows while she was working on her jewelry designs. And Hugo *was* hot. Black wavy hair and eyes that seemed to look into your soul.

"Sure." Stefan shrugged. "I did some work for him a while back."

Penelope inclined her head. "Bodyguard or legal work?"

"Can't divulge client information," he said, wagging a finger at her. "But he's a good guy." He followed Elena's gaze. "Looks like he's with someone tonight, though."

Hugo had his arm around a slender, naturally attractive young woman. They were all laughing at something Elijah was saying.

Elena sighed dramatically. "Another time, then."

Penelope grinned at her friend. "At least you could meet him. Bet his girlfriend would love your work." She jerked her thumb at Stefan. "He's not the only one with connections. Follow me." Before Elena could say another word, Penelope sashayed along the poolside in rhythm with the music, stopping to tap Hugo on the shoulder.

"Hey, Hugo, I've got someone here I'd like you to meet." She turned to Elena, who seemed suddenly speechless. "She really loves your show. Elena's a good friend and one of the hottest jewelry designers around. You should see her shop on Robertson. It's near the Ivy, right next to Fianna Fitzgerald's boutique."

"Um, hi," Elena said.

"Hey, any friend of Penelope's—" Hugo paused when he saw Stefan and gave him a bro hug. "And my man Stefan is a friend, too."

When Hugo shook Elena's hand and kissed her on the cheek, Penelope thought her friend was going to go all fangirl on him and melt, but to her credit, she recovered quickly.

"Come by my shop anytime," Elena said, including his young girlfriend in the conversation.

The girl said, "I know your store and love your work." She held up her wrist to show off a thin platinum bracelet with tiny diamonds Elena had designed. "I'm Alex, by the way. And this is my friend Nora and cousin Elijah," she added, introducing another girl who looked like she was in high school and who was with the other up-and-coming actor.

Elena inclined her head. "You look so familiar…"

Nora shrugged. "You were just talking to my aunt Jen. Everyone says we look alike."

"Or maybe you've seen her in one of the tabloids. The paps have been flocking around us with my upcoming movie and show." Elijah wrapped his arms around Nora and kissed her cheek.

"They're awful lately," Elena said, nodding, glancing at Penelope.

Penelope touched Elena's arm. "If you're okay here, I'm going to look for Lele Rose."

"She's great here," said Hugo, glancing around. "I've got a couple of friends around that Elena might want to meet."

Alexandra giggled and whispered to Elena. "He's got the hottest friends."

Satisfied that Elena was going to have a good time, Penelope peered over the growing crowd that seemed intent on having fun and meeting the most fashionable people around.

She threw a look over her shoulder at Stefan. He was acting better than she'd expected, and she growing tired of sparring with him. Or maybe it was the champagne. "Guess you're coming with me?"

"That's my job."

"I wish you'd quit saying that."

"But it's true."

She blew a wisp of hair from her forehead in exasperation. "I thought by now we could have a different relationship."

Stefan stopped. "What exactly do you mean by that?"

Put on the spot, Penelope groped for words. What *did* she want from him? She wished she could roll back the years and start over with him, but it was too late for that. Monica would always be a thorn between them now.

Stefan was still staring at her, his hands on his hips. "Well?"

"Why can't we just be friends?" Right now, she felt too vulnerable for anything more than that. With her safety and her career at stake, it would be far too easy to let Stefan swoop in and save her. And once she started trusting him again, how long would it be before he did the same thing with someone else as he'd done with Monica? One thing Penelope couldn't abide was disloyalty in friends, lovers, and business partners.

Stefan's face closed off like a mask had been placed over his emotions. "We'll see about that. Right now, you're my client." He clasped her upper arm. "You need to talk to Lele Rose. Let's go."

Penelope bristled. There was no understanding that man. What did he expect from her? She made her way toward Lele, avoiding the older men who gawked as she passed. She was not interested in dating men of her father's generation.

With the music blasting now, Stefan leaned in to her. "So, who's Kristo?"

138

"What, are you *jealous?*" That was it. "On second thought, why don't *you* go?"

Stefan pulled her close to him, holding her gaze with his intense blue eyes. "Are you firing me again?"

"You got it. This time, try to make it stick." She shoved him off and stalked away.

14

"LELE," PENELOPE CALLED, striding away from Stefan. She had important work to do, and he would get in her way. Her career was on the rails careening out of control, and she had to seize every opportunity to resuscitate it.

The eccentric designer held her arms open wide in greeting. "Doll! How I've missed you!"

Lele's glittery red hair swung around her as she hugged her. She wore a leopard print onesie that plunged to a V in the front with sparkly red tights and leopard spiked heels, and she still had the legs to pull it off.

"You're looking good, Lele," Penelope said.

"Not bad for just turning forty," Lele said with a wink, and then turned serious. "I hear you're having a tough time, doll. The fancy New York and French designers have been dropping you."

Penelope tilted her chin up. "That's true, but I was planning on making a career change anyway."

"You're a smart girl, I know you will. And unlike those snobby designers, you're welcome on my runway anytime. This is L.A., and if people ain't talking about you, you ain't nothing."

She clasped Lele's hands in appreciation. "Have any shows coming up?"

"As a matter of fact, I do. A lavish charity affair at the new Waldorf Astoria hotel in Beverly Hills. I'll have my assistant call your agent." Lele leaned toward her. "And unlike most of the shmucks in this town, I really mean it."

That's why Penelope liked Lele. "I have another favor to ask, too."

"Name it. You've always done good work for me."

"I hear you've been working with the studios. I have an idea for a television show that I'd like to pitch."

"That's a great idea, but it's tough to break in." Lele thought for a moment. "I know a producer I could introduce you to." She pulled out her phone and tapped the screen a few times. "Here, I'm sending you one right now. Cynthia is tough, but she's at a new company and I know she's under a lot of pressure to find new shows. Tell her I referred you." She snapped her phone off. "And that's the way I do business. No time to wait around."

Penelope opened her phone, ignoring more messages from Kristo. "Got it." That's one reason why she liked Lele; she was a woman of action, not talk. There were too many talkers in Hollywood.

"Something else I should tell you, too," Lele said. "I'm not one to gossip, but I overheard a conversation at a party that Aimee Winterhaus hosted. I know you and Monica Graber were friends."

"I don't see much of Monica anymore." Penelope had learned to be diplomatic in business. Aimee Winterhaus was the

Fashion News Daily editor she'd last seen in New York.

"I'm aware of that. She was talking to another model—I don't know who she was—about the shooting incident in New York. Said she was sorry the shooter had missed you, but you wouldn't get away next time. She seemed to think you were the root cause of her declining career."

"Monica took care of that all by herself."

"I'm not blind. But she also said you were the cause of her divorce."

Penelope's lips parted in astonishment. "No way, I never even—"

Lele held up a hand. "We both know she's a jealous bitch, lazy as hell, and was only looking for a husband who could support her so she'd never have to work again. When her husband quit his lucrative law practice, she had a fit."

"There were reasons for that," Penelope said softly.

"Hell, I can't blame him. Representing rich, murdering low-lifes? No thanks." Lele brushed her shoulder off for emphasis. "But there are plenty of girls like Monica around, and I've watched them for years, so it doesn't surprise me. There are lots of old goats who'll give someone like her exactly what she wants. And they deserve what they get in return. Nothing but whining about 'why do they listen to all this old music?' What do they expect?" Lele blew a puff of air between her crimson lips.

Penelope chuckled. "Sometimes it's a true love match."

"Rare, but it happens, I guess. Anyway, watch out for Monica."

They chatted a little longer about other designers they knew and the highlights of the current collections. Lele promised to contact her agent again, and then other people descended upon Lele, so Penelope gave her a hug and moved on.

A server whisked by, offering red wine. "Cabernet?

"Absolutely," Penelope said. After taking a glass, she moved to a quiet corner overlooking the city, contemplating her next move. She had to do her homework first, but she could find a lot of information on the Internet. She'd already explored how to pitch a show, and what the show bible—as the show description, synopsis, and episode outlines were called—should contain.

As she sipped her wine, several ideas were running through her mind. A behind-the-scenes look at the runway business, or a reality show, or a travel-lifestyle show. She wasn't wild about the reality show idea, though she suspected that would have a lot of appeal because of what she was going through right now. Yet, she didn't want to capitalize on misfortune, and she needed to make the right move for her long-term career.

She stood gazing out at the twinkling lights, relishing this moment alone. She loved Elena like a sister, but she also enjoyed having time to think. And with any luck, she'd seen the last of Stefan.

Sipping her wine, she wondered why Stefan was so interested in Kristo. She had to admit, Kristo had gone overboard on the flowers, and he'd been sending quite a lot of texts asking her to join him again on his yacht.

Kristo was getting more effusive with each text—*You're gorgeous! Let's go to Monaco! I love you! Let's sail into the sunset!*—

but she knew that was just his socially inept way of complimenting her. Men like that were generally harmless.

Cradling a glass of Perrier, Stefan watched Penelope from a shadowed area just far enough away that she wouldn't notice him. He'd been in his business long enough to know that the people he worked for were under a tremendous amount of pressure, and when they felt threatened by forces beyond their control, they often lashed out.

Penelope was doing just that. Feeling physically endangered, losing work, and being shunned—all these pressures mounted on people. He understood her need for a brief respite. His new phone buzzed and he drew it from his pocket, never taking his eyes off Penelope.

With a wireless earpiece in one ear, he shifted the phone to the other side. "What's up?" It was Josh. He listened for a moment. "Thanks for checking on that. Shouldn't be much longer."

He secured the earpiece to continue monitoring Penelope and Lele's conversation. Before Penelope stormed off, he'd activated the device he'd attached to her purse. She might have fired him—again—but he as far as he was concerned, he was still on assignment. This wasn't the first time a client had fired him when the pressure got to them. They'd apologize and ask him back, though he'd never really left.

Breathing in, he filled his lungs with the cool night air. The female bodyguard he'd been trying to arrange for him had just accepted an extremely lucrative job in the Middle East with a sheikh for his wife and children. He couldn't blame the woman, but he knew Penelope would be upset.

Out of the corner of his eye, he saw Lele Rose throw her head back in laughter. He shook his head. She had to be the most creatively dressed person here tonight. He didn't know her, so he couldn't judge the veracity of her claim she made about Monica, but it wouldn't surprise him.

Monica was highly vindictive, and she'd often blamed Penelope for jobs that she had lost, though Monica had only put in minimal effort. She'd show up late for gigs and didn't really care about her career. More and more, she'd either stay in a separate bedroom or take off on a sudden, unplanned trip. He knew that she was having affairs, but he'd given up caring a long time ago.

He continued listening to the conversation between Lele and Penelope and then watched Penelope get a glass of wine and walk to the edge of the party.

When Monica had told him about the baby, he'd felt a strong sense of duty. His own father had been absent much of the time, and no matter what relationship he might have with Monica, he owed it to his child to be a better father. He'd wrestled with mixed feelings about his father for years and it had taken a lot of therapy to get past it. He didn't want to make the same mistake with his children.

After Monica had lost the baby, everything changed between them. He thought she was acting out her distress, but it turned out that was just the way she was. She was slovenly and seemed to live on lettuce and vodka. So in addition to his full-time work, he picked up after her, did the grocery shopping, cooked, and washed clothes. The only items she would shop for were clothes and alcohol.

They had gone to marriage counseling—his idea—but the therapist had told him there was little he could do in dealing with a bipolar woman at her level unless she agreed to take medication, which Monica steadfastly refused. In the end, he felt he had done as much as he could for her. He had no regrets over his relationship with Monica, which was firmly in the past.

He watched Penelope sip her wine. Moonlight touched her bare shoulders, and he felt his gut tighten. What he regretted was how his relationship with Penelope had ended. Though in his heart, it had never ended. This time, he'd committed to seeing it through. No matter how she treated him, he would bide his time.

She had a right to be angry with him, and he accepted full responsibility for his actions. He also knew that she might never trust him or love him again, but he had to try.

Seeing his friend Hugo approach Penelope, he adjusted his earpiece so he could hear. Penelope would go ballistic if she knew he was monitoring her conversations, but it was part of his job. Even if she would never have him again, he had a duty toward her, particularly in light of Lele's comment about Monica. He made a mental note to check that out.

And Kristo of the thousand flowers, whoever that was. He smirked to himself. The guy was way too obvious.

He thought back to Monica's comment, which sounded extreme, even for her, but he'd learned to never put anything past people. He'd seen plenty of seemingly rational people go berserk, especially when money, sex, drugs, and alcohol were mixed into the equation.

Hugo began talking. Listening, Stefan heard him tell Penelope he was glad that he'd run into her again, and thanked her for introducing him to Elena. He said he was going to stop by Elena's shop to pick up something special for his mom's birthday. Stefan smiled to himself. Good guy, that Hugo.

Stefan continued to observe from the shadows while Penelope sipped her wine. Her every movement transfixed him, from the graceful way she held her wine glass, to the naturally determined tilt of her head. *What made people fall in love?* he wondered. But he'd fallen in love with Penelope the first moment he'd met her.

He'd been no one, a nobody, just another Navy SEAL leaving the world of combat behind and wondering what to do next with his life. He'd had lofty goals. But none of them compared to having a woman he could laugh with, trust, and believe in. In her eyes, he saw the best version of himself reflected.

He blinked hard against the sudden moisture that gathered in his eyes. How often he'd wish that he'd never met Monica. Yet he was a pragmatic man. He would never give up on the woman he loved. In a room full of beautiful women, Penelope was the only one for him.

She drained her wine glass and turned around. Stefan stepped back into the shadows, watching as she headed toward Elena. *Ready to go?* he heard her say. She called Josh on his cell phone, and he heard him promise to meet her outside and then drop off Elena at her home. On their way to the elevator, the two women stopped to say goodbye to Eva Devereaux.

After the elevator doors closed, he strode to the stairwell and took the stairs down. By the time they emerged from the hotel, he was sitting in the front seat next to Josh.

Looking surprised, Josh said, "Where are the two women?"

Stefan nodded toward the pair coming out the door.

"Why weren't you with them?"

"I got fired."

Josh snorted. "Yeah, right. Again."

The two men exchanged a grin before Josh got out to escort Penelope and Elena to the SUV and open their doors.

15

"WHAT DO YOU mean, the woman you promised me can't come?" Penelope had fired him at the club and had only tolerated his continued presence because she thought the female bodyguard would be there the next day.

What a morning. It wasn't even seven and she hadn't had her coffee yet, and Stefan was telling her that the woman had quit. She narrowed her eyes at him. "Are you making this up?" Even as the words came out of her mouth, she knew he wasn't. Stefan wasn't like that.

"I can send someone else for you." Stefan had just arrived to relieve Josh, who been on duty all night. He hooked his thumbs into the belt loops on his blue jeans, waiting for her to respond.

Penelope sighed. "No, you can stay today." Why did he have to look so enticing? Padding barefoot across the cool tile floor to make coffee, she could've sworn a smile crossed his face, but when she looked back, his piercing blue eyes were all business.

"We have a lot of work to do today." Stefan leaned against the counter. "Security system, exterior cameras, changing locks and key codes—"

"Can I get some coffee first?" Penelope drew a breath, the cloying scent of hundreds of flowers in her cozy home proving nearly overwhelming. She'd woken to the incessant buzzing of messages from Kristo—*Miss you a zillion! Come have another Aquavit! Were there enough flowers?!*—so she'd called him to thank him for the bouquets. He told her that his Master's Revenge game was going on sale soon and he'd be coming to Los Angeles. Would she meet him in Marina del Rey? She'd politely declined, saying that she'd probably be working away from the city then.

The sound of a drill outside her window grated on her nerves. Just as she was reaching for the coffeemaker, her phone vibrated. It was an urgent message from Elena. She opened the link in the text and groaned.

As she and Elena had conjectured, the photo of her wielding a baseball bat and wearing a lacy bra while racing after the photographer had hit the tabloid press. It was being shared all over social media with the headline: *Supermodel Goes Beserk!*

Stefan peered over her shoulder. "I thought that was a pretty good action shot when I saw it this morning. You're trending at number one on Twitter, you know."

Horrified, Penelope threw him a menacing look. Was there any part of her life that wasn't going to be exposed as social media fodder?

Holding up his palms to her, Stefan backed away. "I'll leave you with that. I need to check on my team. They're starting work on the exterior cameras." He rapped his knuckles on the counter and left.

A little while later, after she'd recovered from the shock, showered, and dressed, she went to see how the new security work on her house was coming along.

Standing outside by the pool, Penelope shielded her face from the sun, watching the work. She understood that her security was lacking, but workmen were crawling all over her house, inside and out, and it unnerved her.

She loved swimming in the evening to relax, and it was good exercise to keep her figure lean and strong for work, but Stefan had insisted that cameras be mounted around the pool area in the back. Who would be watching her? she wondered. It seemed a little creepy.

She shrugged. Better than dead, she supposed. "Can't they mount that camera a little to the left?"

From his position on the ladder, Stefan said, "We're trying to mount them in the most aesthetically pleasing areas, but they've got to be pointed in specific directions at appropriate intervals so that there's full coverage. That's the only way we can track your movements."

"*My* movements? What about the perpetrators?" Penelope stepped back inside and slammed the door. Rubbing her arms, she tried to calm her nerves. She just felt so violated and was finding it hard not to lash out.

Pulling herself together, Penelope made her way to her office. She had more important things to do, like trying to earn the money to pay for the improvements going on outside. Glancing at her phone, she pondered the contact that Lele Rose had forwarded to her last night.

"No time like the present," she muttered.

To her surprise, ten minutes later she had an appointment scheduled for that afternoon. Hurriedly, she opened her laptop and began to type notes for her show ideas. At the top of the page in bold letters she typed: Behind the Runway.

Penelope searched online for ideas of what to include in her show treatment, growing increasingly excited over prospects. She thought about the designers and models she could interview; she imagined taking a camera backstage at the runway shows and into the designer workrooms; she even added an idea about following struggling young designers and models who showed particular promise.

By the time she was through, she had a slick four-page presentation with photographs. She hadn't felt this optimistic about a project in ages. For the first time since the shooting had occurred, she felt light and happy. She would have a future after all, she decided.

Out of habit, she opened the door to the garage. When an alarm shrilled loudly in response, she jumped and pressed her hands over her ears. "What the hell?"

Stefan raced around the corner and stopped as soon as he saw her. "Going somewhere?"

Later that afternoon, Penelope sat in Cynthia Gibson Marshall's office in the Golden Triangle area of Beverly Hills. She was dressed in one of her more conservative Akris dresses with a draped jacket, and was eager to share her ideas with Cynthia, who had been keen to see her as soon as she'd called. Lele had told her

Penelope would be calling. Projecting into the future, Penelope imagined how well her ideas would be received and how soon they might begin working together.

A middle-aged woman dressed in an Armani jacket with blue jeans and the highest winged Giuseppe Zanotti heels, Cynthia was telling her about the projects they were producing for network and cable television. She stopped in midsentence, looking behind Penelope. "Here's my partner, Jonathan Butler."

A young man, who didn't look as old as she was, stepped inside the spare, antiseptic office. "Hey, how you doing?" Without waiting for an answer, he began pulling out photos of her from the tabloids and spreading them across Cynthia's desk. "Now here's the way I see this show—"

"I have some ideas of my own," Penelope interjected.

"We're very excited about the idea of a reality show for you." Cynthia spread her hands out in the air, mimicking a marquee. "Supermodel Under Siege."

Jonathan hitched up his slacks around his skinny frame, picking up on Cynthia's enthusiasm. "We can send a crew out tomorrow morning and start shooting. If you get any more threats…" he paused and glanced at Cynthia. "Hell, we should plant some right away."

Cynthia shrugged. "Why not?" She turned to Penelope. "You can act shocked and upset, can't you?"

"I won't have to act." With each word coming out of their mouths, she was growing more and more uncomfortable.

"Surely you know there's more acting in reality shows than actual reality." Cynthia rose from her chair and splayed her hands on the desk. "You do have an agent, don't you? I want to talk to him right away and let's get this deal hammered out."

"Her," Penelope said. "But I have a different idea. I call it Behind the Runway and it will focus on the true stories behind the most talented designers and models in the industry."

Penelope quickly placed the printouts on top of the awful photos that Jonathan had dredged up. All at once, she jerked her hand back. There in front of her was a police photograph taken of the gruesome picture she had found in her bathroom just yesterday. "Where did you get this?" She picked up the picture and shook it at the pair.

"It wasn't cheap, let me tell you." Cynthia arched a thinly drawn eyebrow. "We got a lot invested in this project already."

"But about my project, Behind the Runway—"

"You don't understand." Cynthia sat down and steepled her fingers in front of her. "The reality show is the *only* show we're willing to do with you. You should thank your lucky stars that lunatic took a shot at you. Otherwise, we wouldn't even be talking."

Penelope sat back in her chair. "But you asked me to come right in today."

Jonathan perched on the edge of Cynthia's desk. "Yeah, because this is a hot topic, duh." He glared at her as though she were stupid.

"Excuse me," Penelope said, uncrossing her legs and standing tall. "Did you just say 'duh'?"

Jonathan looked comically perplexed. "Yeah, du-uh." He waved his hands for emphasis.

"We're not in the market for a sweet little show about how wonderful all your model and designer friends are." Cynthia added a hearty guffaw at the end. "Controversy sells. Everyone else is making truckloads of money off of your bad luck, so why shouldn't you?"

"Sorry, my bad luck isn't for sale." Penelope could hardly believe what she was hearing. When the pair in front of her didn't respond, she spun on her heel and marched out.

As she strode toward the elevators, she could hear Cynthia and Jonathan laughing and calling her little miss innocent Pollyana. Her face flushed, and she felt a lump forming in her throat. She jabbed the elevator button half a dozen times. Unwilling to wait, she threw open the door to the stairwell and clomped down to the marbled lobby.

Stefan was waiting for her with his arms folded and a smile of encouragement on his face. "How'd it go?"

She pushed past him. "Let's get out of here."

He caught up with her. "Hey, are you okay?"

She stopped and whirled around. "Does it look like I'm okay? That was the most despicable, degrading business meeting I've ever had. The only reason that producer was interested in me is because of the horrible issues going on right now. They even wanted to plant threats, because obviously I'm not suffering enough, nor am I in enough danger."

"Welcome to Hollywood," he replied.

"Jokes, really? At a time like this? You have no taste or sympathy whatsoever." She started off again, and Stefan grabbed her hand.

"Yes, I do. Get in the car. I'll take you somewhere you can relax."

She shrugged him off. "I don't want to go anywhere with you."

"Well, *I'm* driving."

"And I can *walk.*"

People were rushing past them to catch the elevator or to leave the building. They were attracting attention with their argument. In her peripheral vision, Penelope saw a few people start to take photos with their phones, but she didn't care. The most personal details of her life had already been splashed across the tabloids. She was being laughed at and objectified, and she had become virtually unemployable.

She strode past him, her high heels striking the marble floor with vengeance.

Stefan caught up with her again and stepped in front of her. "You think I don't understand what you're going through right now. I do, and I sympathize with you. My job is to protect you, not just physically, but mentally, too."

All at once, the stress of her situation overwhelmed her, and a sob burst forth from deep within her.

"Then get me out of here now," she cried, anxiety twisting her into knots inside. She yearned to feel his arms around her, comforting her, yet she also hated him for being a part of this insane world where they could no longer just be themselves. "If you ever cared for me, take me away from all this."

16

Mammoth Lakes, California

STEFAN WHIPPED ONTO the Interstate 5 Highway heading north out of Los Angeles. He glanced over at Penelope, who sat huddled in the passenger seat, her head still pressed into her hands.

"I have a place five hours from here," Stefan said. "It's quiet and secluded, and I promise the paparazzi can't find you there."

Still clutching her face, Penelope only whimpered.

"Shall I take that as a yes?" Stefan rubbed her arm.

She nodded.

Stefan threaded the SUV through heavy traffic with an expert eye. He'd made a snap decision, but he knew a person could hold up only so long under intense pressure. Even some of his buddies, highly trained Navy SEALs, had reached eventual breaking points. As soon as he saw the warning signs, he'd learned to diffuse the situation.

Touching her arm again to comfort her, he said, "It's going to be okay, just relax."

He knew Penelope well enough to know the strength of her spirit. The fact that she didn't even care where he was taking her, and hadn't even asked, was another sign that she'd reached her threshold.

She'd shared her childhood history with him, and it wasn't as happy as the version she shared with the media. Beneath her artistically glamorous exterior, Penelope was a private person. While she was growing up, her mother had battled depression and anorexia. Her father worked long hours, so she was often left alone to care for her mother, even as a young child. Penelope had told him that after she'd left home, she'd learned more about her mother's condition and sought help for her.

That evening in New York he'd listened to Penelope's speech, and he knew it came from a deeply personal place. Penelope was one of the most genuine-hearted people he'd ever known. It pained him to see others intent on hurting her—Monica included. He glanced across at her and saw that she had dozed off. *That's for the best,* he thought. She was working hard to recreate her life.

Traffic lightened when he turned onto the 395 toward Mammoth Lakes, California. This was a part of the state he loved. He slowed to look for the Tule elk that inhabited this area of the vast Owens Valley. Peering to the east, he saw antlers bobbing across a meadow where the herd was grazing.

These elk, they'd made a comeback, too, he thought.

From a population of half a million, the elk population had declined until they were thought extinct in the 1800s. A breeding pair was found, and a small herd had been relocated to this area just a few decades ago.

He pulled to the side of the road to watch them. It was a simple pleasure and ritual he had, one of many that formed his memories of this region.

Penelope stirred. "Where are we?"

"About halfway there." He brushed her hair from her forehead.

"Hmm." She turned away and went back to sleep.

Before taking off again, he tapped a quick message to Josh. *Find out who Kristo is.* Was the guy an extreme romantic or was he dangerous? *Where's Monica?* Did she know anything? And finally, *Any news from New York?* Phone service was spotty in the Sierras. If the weather was bad, he might be off the grid for a few days, but Josh could make headway in his absence.

Stefan wheeled back onto the road and continued driving. An early snowfall had already dusted the peaks of the mountains that ran on either side of the Owens River Valley. The Sierra Nevada mountain range ran to the west, and the White Mountains rose to the east.

He'd been coming to this part of California since he was a little boy. He slowed again as he passed Lake Crowley, where he'd often gone trout fishing with his father. It was still too early in the season for the lake to be frozen, but it wouldn't be long.

Penelope stirred again when he slowed to the speed limit as they passed through the town of Bishop before beginning the long incline that would carry them into Mammoth Lakes, a village nestled in the Sierra Nevada Mountains at nearly eight thousand feet above sea level. The nearby ski mountain rose another three thousand feet, and it was one of his favorite places to ski in California.

The road to his cabin had been cleared of snow, and it was still early in the season, but that could change overnight. When the cabin came into view, his mood instantly improved. He rolled down his window to let the crisp air flow onto his face. The scent of pine trees and fresh snowfall filled the air. He pulled the SUV to a stop in front of a log cabin and cut the engine.

Stefan sat still, appreciating the silence. Overhead, birds squawked and squirrels scurried through the trees. He loved being surrounded by nature. Reaching out, he ran his hand along Penelope's arm. "Hey, sleepy head, we're here."

"Mmm." She stretched in the seat. Sitting up, she glanced outside and her eyes widened. "Mountains, snow. Where are we?"

"At my parents' cabin in Mammoth Lakes. Well, mine now." He cranked the brake. Not a day went by that he didn't miss his parents, both of whom died far too early.

"What?" She folded her arms around her torso. "It's freezing up here. Are you crazy? I haven't got a thing to wear."

"My mom had some clothes here that will probably fit you. She was tall, too. Whatever else you need, we can buy. Come on."

She gazed at him, and at last, a smile grew on her face. "Thanks for getting me out of L.A."

"That's what you wanted, wasn't it?"

She nodded, and then stepped from the SUV into the soft fallen snow that surrounded the cabin. Tilting her head up, she held her arms out and rotated slowly to avoid slipping in her heels, her eyes on the sky. "It's incredible up here. I'm free, I'm free." She started laughing, and then sank to her knees against a snowdrift, tearing up again as she had in the office building before they'd left Beverly Hills.

Stefan raced to her side. "Hey, it's okay. Let's get inside so you can lose those high heels." She was displaying all the classic signs of prolonged stress. He pulled her to her feet. "Have you been sleeping okay?"

"Hardly at all since New York."

"You'll have a chance to catch up here."

They climbed the steps, and Stefan opened the door. Like the exterior, natural logs comprised the interior of the cabin. A fireplace anchored one side of the rustic living area, and the kitchen spread out on the other. It was a modest place, but he liked it. There were two bedrooms, each one with a fireplace.

"You'll find some warmer clothes in the closet. Help yourself." He took an old teapot from the stove and filled it with water. Striking a match, he lit the burner and adjusted the flame.

A few minutes later, Penelope emerged wearing jeans and a red plaid flannel shirt with a funny look on her face. "I feel like a lumberjack."

Pouring hot water into two cups of cocoa, he looked up and grinned. *A gorgeous lumberjack,* he thought to himself.

She held out a foot. "I found some old boots."

"Glad they fit. Looks like you wear the same size Mom did." He scooted a mug of hot cocoa toward her. "This should warm you."

Penelope slid onto a wooden stool and picked up the mug.

161

"Did your wife—"

"Ex. Never came here. Too remote for her taste." He pulled a cranberry red wool sweater his mother had knitted for him over his shirt and pushed up the sleeves. "I'll build a fire shortly. Have to bring in some wood."

"So what do you do up here?"

"Are you kidding?" Stefan laughed. "You've been living in Hollywood too long." He sipped his cocoa, studying her over the rim of his mug. She seemed to relax a little, but he could see dark smudges beneath her fatigue-rimmed eyes that he hadn't noticed before. She'd probably been covering the dark circles with makeup.

"I'm serious," she said. "Do you ski?"

"Sure. Downhill, cross country, snowboard. In the summer, there's great fishing, hiking, and mountain biking."

"Swimming?"

"In the lakes. Pretty cold, though. Snow melts from the mountains." He pushed the drapes open, revealing snowy mountain views. When he turned around, she was staring into the distance, her chin cupped in her hand.

"Think I'll ever have a normal life again?"

Stefan shrugged. "If that's what you want, why not?"

"When I saw all the cameras going up around the house, I began to feel claustrophobic. I can't step outside with people snapping photos."

"You can here."

Penelope sipped her cocoa. "I couldn't live in a place like this."

"It's your choice." When she looked doubtful, he said, "Really, it's a choice you can make. At any time, you can walk away. What could you get for your house in the Hollywood Hills?"

Penelope nodded thoughtfully.

"You're feeling like people have control over you. In a sense, they do. But you can change that. I just wanted to show you that you still have the power to make choices in your life."

"That sounds like the lawyer in you talking."

He laughed and stretched his hands to clasp hers. "I want you to know that you're safe here, and I have no expectations of you. I brought you here to recuperate. L.A. is a pressure cooker for high profile people. You needed a break."

She raised her eyes to his. "How'd you become so wise?"

"Just learned a few things along the way." He drained his cocoa. "Need to get some firewood."

Leaving her inside, he stepped out to collect firewood he'd split the last time he was here. He filled his arms, wondering if this visit would be the complete undoing of them, or if it would bring them closer.

Perhaps he had been selfish in bringing her here, but at that moment in the hotel lobby when she'd pleaded with him to get her out of there, this cabin was the only thought that entered his mind. He'd never brought a client here before. Or any other woman.

Stomping snow from his shoes, he thought about Josh, hoping he would have some answers to his text when they returned. Suspicions simmered in his mind. Who would stand to benefit

from Penelope's death? Or from the media circus that surrounded it?

17

"SMELLS DELICIOUS." PENELOPE perched on a wooden stool, watching Stefan make dinner. A fire crackled in the stone fireplace, chasing the chill from the log cabin. She rubbed her hands together to warm them.

"Just your standard mountain fare." Over a searing heat on the old stovetop, Stefan quickly stirred vegetables in a battered wok, added Chinese sauces and spices, and then turned them out over a bed of brown rice and quinoa.

She laughed. "Hardly. I thought you'd be eating biscuits and gravy and a slab of venison up here."

"Not anymore." He made a face. "Healthy body, healthy mind."

"What else have you got in here?"

"Help yourself," he said, nodding toward the refrigerator.

Opening the freezer, she exclaimed. "You're well stocked. Cherry Garcia *and* Chunky Monkey. Guess you can't be all good all the time."

"Ice cream soothes the soul. And it's great with baked apples."

"That sounds yummy. Have any apples?"

"Frozen, like the vegetables. For anything fresh this time of year, we have to go to the market. Friends have gardens after the thaw, but I'm not here often enough. The one year I tried it, the wildlife ate better than I did." He slid two steaming plates across the sturdy wood bar, poured wine, and pulled up a stool. "Bon appétit." He clinked her wine glass.

"This mountain man lifestyle is a lot more glam that I thought."

"Then you can split the next batch of firewood."

She swept her hair back. "Sure, I'll give it a try." When she caught him grinning at that, she pressed her lips together. "You'd be surprised at what I can do." When they'd left the city, she'd been distraught over the incident at the producer's office, but now, having slept on the way, she felt her energy returning.

"I haven't forgotten. You're an amazing woman, Penelope. What's happening to you right now isn't fair."

His brilliant blue eyes caught the firelight, and she remembered how she'd once thought she could stare into those eyes forever. She averted her gaze and picked up the chopsticks he'd laid out. "You know me. I'm not one to whine about things not being fair."

"Always liked that about you. How we deal with the unfairness life lobs at us is the true test of our character."

"I've always prided myself on being a strong person, but lately I feel like I'm cracking under pressure." She slid her hand across the bar and squeezed his hand. "I've said things to you I regret, and I'm sorry."

"Being a strong person doesn't mean being strong all the time." He lifted their entwined hands to his lips and kissed her fingertips. "Humans need intervals of time away from stress for periodic recovery. Builds resilience, the ability to bounce back from stressful situations."

"That makes sense, counselor." Movement through the window caught her eye. "Look, it's snowing."

"That happens a lot here."

She poked him with a chopstick. "Don't be a smart ass."

"Those aren't weapons. Eat the dinner I slaved over for you."

Penelope laughed. What a day she'd had. Her emotions had run the gamut, from the high of landing a meeting with a producer to the lowest dejection. Stefan was right; she was mentally exhausted and needed a respite.

As they ate and talked, Penelope remembered how it used to be between them, when he was in law school and she was climbing the rungs of her career ladder. They'd both had dreams, but life had intervened and it hadn't been fair. As he'd said, over the years she had become more resilient, but had she recovered enough to give their relationship another chance?

After dinner, Penelope helped him wash the dishes, and then they sat in front of the fireplace and played Scrabble, a game they'd both liked to play years ago.

Rearranging her last letters—S, L, K, E, R, E—she raised her eyes to Stefan and smiled.

"*Elsker.*" She placed all her remaining tiles on the board game and said, "*Voilà.*"

Stefan lifted an eyebrow. "Danish? No fair."

Laughing, she folded up the game. "Let's go to bed." She didn't mention that the word meant 'love.'"

Stefan guided her to the larger bedroom and showed her where everything was. "Get a good night's sleep," he said. "You've got a lot of wood chopping to do in the morning."

When Penelope woke the next morning, she pushed the drapes aside and gazed outside, struck by the beauty of fresh fallen snow against a blue crystalline sky. She pulled on a thick flannel robe and tucked her bare feet into furry slippers she found in the closet.

Shuffling into the living area, she saw Stefan outside on the porch on his phone, his breath forming puffs in the cold air. The coffeemaker was just finishing its brew, so she poured two cups, stirred in creamer, and took them outside.

"Then her house will be ready by the time we return." His face lit up when she handed him a cup of coffee made exactly as she knew he liked it.

He clicked off the phone and turned to her. "My team is still working on the installation of your security system. The cameras are in place and functioning, and there have been no more incidents at your house."

Penelope wrapped her hands around the coffee cup to warm them. "I suppose that's good, under the current circumstances."

"Once the police find the perpetrator, the media storm should die down. I've got Josh following up on that."

"Think they're still working on my case? New York's a tough city."

"They've got a good force there." He swiveled toward her, his eyebrows drawn together. "Is there anything else you can think of that might be helpful to the police?"

Penelope shook her head. "I wish I could."

"I don't mean to upset you, but could Monica have anything to do with it?"

"What on earth...?" *Why would he ask about Monica? What could she have to do with what happened in New York?* Other than seeing Monica there—and that certainly wasn't out of the ordinary—she couldn't think of anything. "Do you think she is jealous enough to have set up a stunt like that in public? For starters, I don't think she's smart enough."

"I had to ask. Let me know if you think of anything. Hopefully, your life can return to normal soon."

"Except that I'm virtually unemployed. Once you're replaced on the runway, it's hard to get back in the lineup, especially at my age."

Stefan leaned against a porch timber and draped his arm around her. She leaned into him, appreciating the warmth of his body against hers.

"That's a tough business you're in," he said. "Have any other ideas?"

"A few, but the producer shot them down."

"You'll keep trying."

"You bet." Penelope leaned her head on his shoulder, watching brown squirrels scampering at the edges of the clearing. "Like those squirrels, I have a few nuts tucked away for cold periods."

She sipped her coffee, thinking. After the disastrous meeting

169

she'd been to yesterday, she'd given more thought to what she could do differently. Producers wanted shows that were sensational, or focused on something new.

Closing her eyes, she inhaled the delicious scents of morning. Coffee, pine, snow...Stefan. She opened her eyes and shivered, reminding herself not to get too comfortable around him. "I've got to get dressed."

"Need anything from town?"

"I've got all I need for chopping wood." She was determined to show him what she was made of.

18

PENELOPE HEFTED THE wood-handled ax over her shoulder and brought it down through the wood with a clean break. She adjusted her thick gloves before stacking the wood she'd split into a neat pile. Picking up the ax, she inhaled a sharp breath of crisp mountain air and brought the blade down again with a resounding crack.

"Bravo," Stefan said, clapping his hands as he crunched through the snow toward her. "I thought you were kidding." He wore a ski jacket and pants and carried a backpack.

"You forgot that my family had a farm when I was young. It gets cold where we lived in Denmark." She kicked the wood to one side and brought the ax down again. "And this is great exercise. Really builds upper body strength."

"Impressive. This is the kind of photo that needs to get out there in the media. An ax is much more menacing than a baseball bat."

She glanced down at her bulky winter clothing. "I think I'd have to shed a few layers for that to trend on Twitter."

Stefan crossed the space behind her and wrapped his arms

around her. His breath was hot against her flushed cheek. "That's enough wood for today. I've got something else I want to show you." He took the ax from her and put it away.

Taking her by the hand, he led her to a shed affixed to the house and creaked open the door, revealing an assortment of cold weather sporting gear. "It's a great morning for cross-country skiing. These should fit you, now that I know you're the same size my mom was." A wistful expression touched his face before he opened a closet and gestured. "Coats, hats, gloves. Whatever you need. Want to join me?"

"Sounds good. I love cross-country skiing." Penelope saw emotion cloud his eyes as he blinked a few times. Stefan had lost both his parents within a year of each other. His mother had died of breast cancer, and his father had a heart attack the following year. He'd always said that his father had died of a broken heart.

Penelope pulled outerwear over her clothes and took the skis and boots. Sitting on a bench inside the shed, she reached down to unlace her boots and exchanged them for ski boots.

Stefan adjusted the pack on his back. Penelope nodded to it and asked, "Are we going to be gone long?"

"Not that long, but around here you never know. Better to be safe and have food, water, and flares in case of an emergency." He peered toward the mountaintop. "Once the snow is heavily packed, there's always the threat of an avalanche. But we get earthquakes up here too, and injuries do occur."

"You have a first aid kit in that backpack?" She walked out of the shed and stepped into her skis.

Beside her, Stefan snapped on his skis and picked up his

poles. "Sure do. I'm pretty handy with splints. There's a lot of crud in the open country. Have to watch for it."

Stefan helped her make sure her skis were properly adjusted, and they pushed off, gliding across the white blanket of snow. Penelope had grown up skiing in Europe—both downhill and off-piste through wild terrain—and she loved the strenuous exercise.

It wasn't long before they were striding on skis through pristine banks of powdery snow and having a thrilling time. Stefan took the lead carving paths through new territory since he knew the area, and then let Penelope lead the way gliding through other existing trails. After a while, she dropped back beside him when the paths were wide enough for the two of them to ski side-by-side.

She couldn't remember when she'd had so much fun with a man. Here in the wilderness, with none of the modern-day stresses around, her spirits soared. She caught a glimpse of what the future with Stefan could be like, and the image in her mind's eye nearly brought her to tears.

Yet this day in the wilderness wasn't real life. Could they survive the stresses and temptations of the big city together? He'd broken her heart the last time, and she didn't know if she was strong enough to try again.

The sun was high in the sky when he swooshed to a stop ahead of her. She ran a finger around her turtleneck, letting cool air bathe her heated neck. "I had no idea we've been skiing as long as we have been. What do you have to eat in your backpack?"

"A surprise." He pointed to a ledge where several boulders protruded from the snowdrift. "We can sit over there."

Following his lead, Penelope removed her skis, brushed off the rocks, and climbed on top of them. The sun was warm on her face and the crisp air cool. This reminded her of ski outings with her parents when she was young, on those rare occasions when her mother was having a good day.

Stefan pulled out a red-checked cloth and spread it on the rock, and then withdrew two thick sandwiches. "Grilled vegetables, parmesan, and prosciutto on Italian bread." He reached inside the pack again and offered her a small bottle of wine. "A split of Tignanello from Tuscany. All we need for lunch. With plastic stemware." He dug deeper, grinning. "And Anthon Berg chocolates from Denmark. A lunch fit for Olympians."

"And here I thought that bag was full of bandages, flares, and granola bars. Where did you get all this?"

His face ruddy from the sun, he stretched his long legs out and flexed them. "I freeze a lot of supplies because you can't always get out to the store up here if there's a heavy snowfall. I've got a deep freeze in the laundry room, so I throw in bread, grilled vegetables, cheese, and fruit. Whatever I might want later. I learned a lot in the Navy."

Penelope peeled back the wrapper on her sandwich and bit into it. "Mmm, this is so good. I didn't realize I was starving."

"Skiing always works up the appetite."

She grinned. "And burns the calories. Even models can eat whatever they want up here and not gain an ounce."

Stefan poured wine for her and they lifted their plastic

glasses. "To the future," he said, his blue eyes rivaling the sun's brilliance.

Penelope caught herself wishing he might be in that future, too. She raised her glass. "The future. May it be as bright and serene as today. *Skål*." Being in Mammoth Lakes was a perfect respite. Los Angeles felt a million miles away.

Stefan gestured toward the highest peak with his glass. "Personally, I find skiing these mountains with you pretty exciting. You're good."

"You forgot that I grew up on skis."

He lowered his glass. "I haven't forgotten a thing, Penelope."

"Neither have I, Stefan." That was the problem. There were parts of their relationship that she wished she could forget.

"Do you think there's a possibility that after this is over, you might consider…"

She grew quiet, waiting for him to finish his sentence.

He coughed into his hand. "Excuse me, must be these pines, the air is thick with them." He took a large bite of his sandwich.

Penelope watched him closely. "What is it you wanted to ask me, Stefan?"

Taking another drink of wine, he looked at her as though he were considering his words. "When I asked you who Kristo was, you didn't answer my question."

"That's what you wanted to ask me?"

"Not that exactly, but that's what I need to know."

"Why?" She took a bite of her sandwich, waiting for his reply.

His face held an earnest expression. "Because we need to investigate people near to you who could mean to hurt you."

"You've got to be kidding. Kristo would never hurt me."

"The flowers, his texts. He's pretty over the top, isn't he?"

Penelope put her sandwich down. "You've been reading my text messages?" Her jaw tightened as she thought of this.

"You hired me to. That's part of it."

"No, you should have asked me first. That's private. And there's nothing unusual about his text messages. He's just socially awkward."

"I'd like to be the judge of that. And to be honest, those messages are excessive. Would you say he might be stalking you?"

She thought for a moment. She'd known other models who'd been the victim of stalking and it was awful. "How could he be a stalker if he isn't even in the same country?"

"Digital stalking," he said with a serious look.

Penelope started laughing. "I won't deny that Kristo is eccentric, but I don't think he's dangerous."

Clearing his throat, he added, "Look, if you're dating him and if it's serious, then I won't hold out hope."

"Is that what this is about? I'm not dating him."

For a man so confident, Stefan looked a little uncomfortable. "Then I could ask you out for dinner sometime?"

"Or you could ask me out to lunch, or to go skiing. You could even ask me to go to your place in Mammoth Lakes." She smiled playfully.

"Now who's the smart ass? I'm being serious." Reaching out, Stefan grabbed her knit cap and mussed her hair.

Penelope started laughing and tried to snatch her cap back, but he dangled it out of her reach with one hand, and then wrapped his other arm around her, pulling her close to him.

She pushed him off the rock and as she did, her cap went flying into a ravine and he started to slide down the snowy side, but not before he reached out and grabbed her, taking her with him.

Together they rolled through the snow, laughing and holding on to each other, trying to stop. When they finally did, Stefan brushed the snow from her lips and cradled her face in his hands. Penelope lifted her eyes to his, seeing passion and restraint in his gaze. Closing her eyes, she brought her mouth to his in a kiss that she hadn't realized she'd wanted so desperately.

After a while, Stefan dragged his lips from her mouth and feathered kisses over her face and neck, warming her cool skin with the heat of his passion.

Penelope pulled him closer again, deepening the kiss they'd shared. She wanted all of him. In the instant that their lips touched, she'd lost her heart to him once again. She could feel the strength of his arousal matching her own.

Stefan slid his arms under her, easily lifting her and brushing snow from her hair. Pulling his own knit cap off, he tugged it over her hair. "Have to keep you warm," he said, his deep voice thick with desire. He lifted her and trudged through the knee-deep snow back to their rocks, where he began to kiss her again.

She wrapped her arms around him and ran her fingers through his thick hair, recalling how he'd felt under her hands.

Finally, he pulled back. "You know we still have to ski out

of here. And this rock is awfully cold and hard."

"Hmm. Think you know a better place?"

"I do. A little cabin full of expertly cut firewood to keep us toasty warm." After another kiss, he raised himself from her and helped her up. "I'll get your skis."

While he did that, Penelope swept the remains of their lunch into the backpack. She glanced up as the sun slipped behind a bank of clouds gathering over the mountains, dropping the temperature a few degrees.

They had skied hard on the way out, but on the return, filled with desire, they both pushed themselves even more. Snow began to drift onto them, coating Stefan's hair, and collecting in the folds of her jacket. She gripped her poles and pushed herself on, taking the lead.

"I know a shortcut," he called out from behind.

With the snow falling more rapidly, Penelope tilted her face down against the flurries.

She slowed to rest and let him pass her. As he glided by, his arms and shoulders straining with effort, he motioned ahead. The snowflakes became plumper and thicker, separating her from Stefan.

She increased her stride on her skis and worked her poles, catching up with him again. The snow was swiftly approaching white-out conditions. Since she didn't know the area, it was imperative that they stay close together.

The snow muffled sound, and the birdsong that had accompanied them on the way was silenced as the birds sought shelter from the snow.

Ahead of her, Stefan disappeared behind a boulder and a stand of trees. She strode on, narrowly missing rocks that jutted out in her path.

She pushed herself to keep up with him, though she could no longer see him. Blinking against the snow, she squinted ahead. A few minutes later, she glanced down. There were no tracks ahead of her.

She'd lost Stefan.

Wiping snow from her eyes, she swung around.

Nothing.

She called his name and waited for a reply.

Silence.

The snow was falling so fast it was covering the tracks she'd just made. She shoved off, trying to follow her own tracks back to the last place she'd seen him, hoping she could see his tracks veer off, unless they'd already been covered with snow.

As she came closer to where she thought she'd lost him, she began to call out his name again. She stopped and listened.

Still silence.

She could no longer see ahead of her. Praying she was heading in the right direction, she strode through the thick snow encasing her in a blanket of white. Panic began to rise in her chest.

Her breath became shallow, and soon she felt light-headed. "No," she said, forcing the word through numb lips. "No, no, no."

She drew deep breaths until she regained control. Brushing snow from her eyes, she put her head down to find her tracks, worried that within minutes, the tracks would disappear from sight.

There wasn't much she could do in blizzard conditions except take shelter. She pressed on, though her old tracks faded until finally, she could no longer see them, or anything around her.

She was lost.

19

"STEFAN, STEFAN!" PENELOPE called his name over and over, but the snow only muffled her words and threw them back to her.

Without the sun overhead, the temperature had dropped and it would be dark soon. She'd skied the groomed slopes of Mammoth's downhill course before, but she'd never been in this remote area of the Sierras. However, she knew the sun set early and with the thick cloud cover, she didn't have much daylight left.

She could ski on, but she was completely turned around now, and she might be heading deeper into the forest. Or she could find shelter and wait it out, conserving her energy until there was a break in the conditions.

But where was Stefan? Was he in the same situation or had he made it home?

She fumbled in her jacket and pants, but it was no use. Her phone was at the cabin, though she probably couldn't get a signal here anyway.

Extreme conditions called for orderly thought. With her

head down against the snow, she leaned against her poles. Very likely Stefan was in as much trouble as she was, but they might end up going in circles looking for each other, and eventually freeze to death. She had to think, and fast.

Stefan had his Navy SEAL training to draw on. Chances were good that he'd fare better than she would.

And he had flares in the backpack.

Once the snow ebbed, he'd send up flares.

Survival training she'd had years ago suddenly sprang to mind. *Shelter in place.* She swung around. But where?

She headed toward a stand of trees. When she got there, she removed her skis and used one to dig a sort of cavern into the snow. It was slow going, because the blizzard was relentless. She pulled her turtleneck up over her mouth and continued to dig. It was an irregular hole in the side of a drift, but it would do.

It was imperative to retain her body heat as long as she could. Recalling her training, she knew if she sat or laid on the snow, she could freeze. She found some broken branches protruding from the snow and yanked on them, flailing in the deepening snow.

One by one she dragged the fallen branches of pine trees she found to the little cave she'd dug. She tossed them inside, forming a bed she could lie on. Darkness was encroaching, and there wasn't much more she could do but wait it out.

Turning back, she stumbled onto another protruding object near a boulder. Picking herself up, she ran her hand along the object, which was too smooth to be a branch.

It was a ski.

She jerked on it. And then she heard a moan.

"Stefan! Stefan!"

Frantically digging, she finally reached him. His hair was frozen, his lips were blue, and he had a nasty gash on his forehead.

She rubbed his face. "Stefan, wake up. Can you hear me?"

His eyes opened, but he struggled to speak. "Penel…my pack."

"Stay with me. Looks like you fell." Peeling off the knit cap he'd given her, she pulled it over his head and folded the brim over his ears to contain what body heat he still had. She kept digging until she reached his pack. Fumbling with the zipper amid the falling snow, she got it open. She held each item up to her face, looking for anything that could help them.

She found it.

An emergency tarp, tightly folded. She unfolded it and spread it around Stefan to keep him warm. Finding hand warmers, she ripped them open with her teeth and shoved them inside his jacket, gloves, and boots. At the bottom on the pack was another thin thermal blanket. She thanked God he was prepared. Her fingers touched his phone, but it was dead.

"Can you walk?"

"Leg…hurt."

His speech sounded slurred, and he seemed confused. She hunched on her heels, thinking. She could dig another cave, or drag him to the one she'd built.

She placed his skis beside him. "I'm going to dig around you and roll you onto this tarp over your skis." He was drifting in and out of consciousness. A few minutes later, she shoved him onto the tarp over the skis, hoisted the backpack, and pushed off.

It worked. With sheer determination, she shoved him toward her little cave. Once she got him there, she rolled him inside on top of the pine branches. After enlarging the opening, she crawled in beside him and wrapped the emergency blanket and tarp around both of them to retain their body heat.

Shivering beside him, she rubbed her hands together to create friction and warmth. Watching the snow continue to fall outside the cave, she wondered how long it would be until they were found.

If they were found.

Penelope cupped Stefan's cold face in her hands. "Can you hear me?"

His eyes fluttered. She ran her hands over his cheeks in an attempt to warm his skin, which felt icy under her touch.

"Stefan, can you hear me?" Frantically she kissed his lips, willing her warmth into him. He was so weak, he could hardly responded.

She choked on a sob at seeing him like this, realizing how important he was to her even after everything they'd been through. "Don't you dare leave me. Not now."

His mouth twitched and she kissed his again, warming his lips with her own. "I love you, I've always loved you. Stay with me. I know you can do it."

She brushed tears from her eyes just as he opened his. "Love…you, too." His lips curved to one side and he drifted off again.

Penelope continued to kiss him and use the friction of her

limbs to warm him. She snuggled closer, praying he would make it. And that they would make it together. But if this was her last night on earth, at least she was with the man she loved, and for that, she was thankful.

Throughout the night, Penelope kept the snow cleared from the entry of their little igloo to avoid a buildup of carbon monoxide. Each time she came back in, she wrapped herself around Stefan to keep him warm. She woke him intermittently to check on him, telling him over and over how much she loved him and imploring him to stay with her.

As morning dawned, the snowfall lessened and Penelope crawled from the cave. Taking a flare in her quivering hands, she activated it. Orange smoke billowed out and up, carried on the wind. It lasted for about a minute. With any luck, it would be seen by a ranger or other emergency personnel. She joined Stefan to wait.

No one came.

She could leave him and ski out for help, or she could try again. There were two more flares.

Opening the package of the second one, she activated it as she had before, but it fizzled out without emitting any smoke. Drawing a breath, she opened the last one with care and set it off.

Smoke spiraled upward on the wind and with it, her prayers that it would be seen. Returning to Stefan, she burrowed beside him to wait. If help didn't come, she'd have to devise another plan. She resolved to get them out as soon as possible.

She'd been turning over new plans in her mind when she heard a distant hum that slowly grew louder. She scrambled from the cavern and spied a vehicle below them. Racing to the edge of the ridge, she waved her arms and screamed as loud as she could.

"Up here, help! Up here!"

Within minutes, an emergency rescue snowmobile roared toward her, and Penelope jumped and yelled with elation.

As the man came to a stop, he called out, "Saw your flare. You okay?"

"I need medical help for him."

The man hurried to them and knelt down at the mouth of her makeshift cave. "Got a toboggan on the back we can put him on. Let's see if he can be moved."

Penelope huddled beside Stefan on his bed at the Mammoth hospital, holding his hand. He was sleeping now.

The emergency room doctor had questioned him, and it was determined that Stefan had probably hit a boulder in the white-out conditions, knocking himself unconscious.

"You very likely saved his life," the doctor told her as he cleaned Stefan's wound and bandaged it. "He's had a mild traumatic brain injury, a concussion. Once we've determined that he's stable, we'll discharge him, but you must keep him quiet for a while." The doctor perused Stefan's chart. "From the looks of him, he's pretty tough. Could have been a lot worse. Will you be able to stay with him?"

"Of course," Penelope said. She wasn't about to leave Stefan's side. During their ordeal, she'd had time to reflect on how important he was to her.

Stefan had showed her that she mattered to him, too, in so

many ways. She thought about that evening in New York. With hundreds of people there, no one else came to her aid. While others scattered for cover, only Stefan had stepped into the line of fire to help her.

And that was after she'd told him she never wanted to see him again years ago.

He'd taken a flight to Denmark to offer his professional services. And he had yet to ask her for money, even though she knew he was outlaying substantial funds and resources to ensure her safety.

Even though she thought he was being nosy about some things, he always had her best interest at heart, despite her complaining.

He rustled in his sleep, and she kissed his cheek. She knew she hadn't been the easiest person to deal with lately.

Besides his concern for her, he did little things that showed he cared. Making meals he knew she liked, remembering her birthdate, wanting her to be safe and comfortable. Whisking her away when the pressure became too great to handle.

She stroked his hand. In so many ways he had shown her that he was worthy of being trusted again.

If she couldn't do that, she realized, then the problem was with her.

Yet feelings of distrust inside her persisted. What was she going to do?

20

"NO ONE RECOGNIZED you in the hospital?" Stefan shifted in his bed as Penelope put a breakfast tray in front of him.

"If they did, no one said anything." She removed a napkin from the tray, revealing the breakfast she'd prepared for him. A grilled vegetable frittata, oatmeal, a blueberry muffin, and a fruit smoothie with protein powder. The man had a well-stocked kitchen.

Stefan pushed himself to a seated position. He wore green plaid flannel pajama bottoms, but his chest was bare. It was as firm and well-defined as she'd recalled. He was an absolutely beautiful specimen of a man. After pausing a moment to enjoy the view, she handed him a robe. "You've got to be hungry."

"On several levels," he said, and gave her a kiss. "I'm not surprised that no one recognized you—or mentioned it. A lot of Olympic athletes live and train here. It's not as glamorous or well-covered as Aspen, so celebrities can visit or live out of the spotlight here." He named off a couple of Oscar and Grammy award winners who lived normal lives in and around the area.

Penelope chuckled, hugging one of his shirts she'd put on

around her. "When we rolled into the hospital, I didn't exactly look like my cover images."

He drew his hands over her slicked back hair and kissed the top of her head. "When I opened my eyes that morning, you were the most the beautiful thing I'd ever seen in my life—frozen hair, runny nose, and all."

"I felt the same way," she said, laughing with him.

As he ate, she glanced out the window. The storm had cleared and snowfall wasn't expected again for days. "It's awfully quiet here." She was enjoying the seclusion of the cabin.

"People tend to stay in when blizzards are predicted." Twisting a side of his mouth up in one of his old grins, he added, "I was so dazzled by you I neglected to check the weather. It moved in awfully fast. That can happen here."

He drank the smoothie and started on the frittata. "Now that there's been a good early snowfall, if it stays cold the downhill skiers and snow boarders will flood the town soon."

As he ate ravenously, Penelope watched with satisfaction. He'd slept through lunch and dinner at the hospital, and had hardly touched the plate they'd left. This was his first real meal since their last lunch together on the mountain.

"Now that I'm proven, maybe I can get on as a bodyguard," she said, teasing him.

He wiggled his fingers. "Not even frostbite. You passed the nature survival test."

"Thanks to the gear in your backpack. I'll never ski without one again." A fresh bandage covered part of his forehead, but other than that, he looked fine. *Extremely fine*, she thought.

After finishing his breakfast, he pushed it to one side and brought her closer to him. "Now, where did we leave off at lunch? As I recall, we were hurrying back for something important." He touched his lips to hers, deepening into a warm, loving kiss.

Embracing him, she kissed him back, running her hands over his stubbled jawline. He felt so masculine, so sexy… She released a moan.

He caressed her face, her neck, her shoulders, filling her with desire she'd missed so much. Easing her down beside him, he rose above her, teasing her with delicious flicks of his tongue.

She wanted more—so much more—but she pressed her hand gently against his chest. "This will to have to wait. The doctor warned you against vigorous exercise."

"It doesn't have to be that vigorous," Stefan said, protesting.

Penelope laughed. "That's not the way I remember it."

She got up to take the tray back, but Stefan caught her hand and pulled her back to him, peppering her face and lips with kisses.

"I remember what you said up there," he said, turning serious. "That meant so much to me. Your words sustained me. I don't know if I could've held on without you. Did you really mean what you said?"

"That I love you?" Penelope sucked in her bottom lip in thought. "I don't think I've ever stopped loving you."

Relief flooded his face, softening the worry lines on his brow. "I feel the same. I've been so ashamed of what I did—"

Penelope pressed a finger to his lips to silence him. "Remember what the doctor said. You're not to get upset."

He nipped her neck and slid a muscular arm around her. "Telling you that I love you will never upset me. Those are the happiest words I can imagine saying."

Wrapping her arms around him, she rocked back and forth as waves of happiness swept over her. These were the words she'd longed to hear again. She closed her eyes, reveling in the moment and thankful for the gift of discovery they'd been given.

How differently yesterday might have turned out. But it hadn't been their time to die. Today was their time to live and love. Today and ever onward, she hoped, for as long as they lived.

Feeling blissful, she left him with a kiss, picked up the tray, and started back to the kitchen. She smiled as she thought of their future together. Decisions would have to be made, but she was confident they could overcome anything now.

As she put the tray down, her phone vibrated on the counter with an incoming call. She'd just plugged it in when they'd arrived home. No one knew the ordeal they'd just survived. She picked up the phone.

"Hi Elena. Sorry I've been out of touch, but you won't believe what happened." Penelope went on to tell her about the blizzard and the ensuing catastrophe.

"I'm relieved to hear that," said Elena. "I was worried when you disappeared, so I called Josh. He told me that Stefan had taken you to Mammoth to de-stress. I know you're not crazy about Stefan, but I think that was a really good idea. I hope you're getting some rest."

"You might say that we called a truce." She couldn't contain the happiness in her voice.

"What do you mean?"

"I mean that we're picking up where we left off a number of years ago. I think we're going to start dating again."

Elena let out a low whistle. "Congrats, but won't Kristo be disappointed to hear that."

"We're going to have to stay here a few more days until Stefan improves."

The sound of Elena's laughter bubbled through the phone. "That sounds like a delicious little love nest."

"You have no idea. He has the best stocked kitchen I've ever seen in a bachelor pad. And he's a fabulous cook."

Elena chuckled again. "That's not exactly what I was talking about."

"But that's exactly what got us in trouble," Penelope said, laughing with her friend. "So, was there a reason you called?"

Elena hesitated before she spoke. "I really hate to give you bad news."

"Is everything okay?" Penelope pressed her hand to her chest.

"It seems that you're trending on social media again."

Penelope felt the air whoosh from her lungs. "Now what?"

"Do you remember when we were on Kristo's yacht, and he showed us a game he was working on? It was called Master's Revenge."

"You mean the one where he'd pasted my head on his character?"

"That would be the one."

Penelope shut her eyes and leaned on the counter for support. "Is it out?"

"It's number one on the gaming chart."

Penelope felt a sense of dread coursing through her. "Oh no, he didn't."

"Oh yes, he did. You're the star."

The nerve of him. "He can't use my likeness without permission, and I sure as hell didn't give it to him."

"Looks like that's what your attorney will have to tell him."

Penelope sighed. Would her problems ever go away? Still, she had to be realistic. As long as she was in the public eye, it was to be expected. Just not from her friends. That is, she'd once thought of Kristo as a friend. A slightly weird friend, but she'd never thought he meant to harm her. He was more like a yapping puppy dog enthusiastically trying get attention. "I'll call Scarlett right away."

She hung up the phone and banged her fist on the counter. "Now what?"

Penelope whirled around. "You should be resting."

"I am resting. But clearly you're not. Tell me what's going on." He crossed the room and enfolded her in his arms.

She'd forgotten how nice it was to be able to share her burdens with someone who cared. Someone who wasn't on her payroll and just wanted the best for her. Her friends were in that category, of course, but Stefan was different. She remembered when they had been a team. A team for life. Could she hope for that again?

"Kristo launched a new video game." With a sinking feeling,

she remembered what Stefan thought about Kristo.

"The man of the thousand flowers?" Stefan gazed at her with concern. "What does that have to do with you?"

She squirmed in his arms and pulled away. "When Elena and I visited him on his yacht in Denmark he showed us a demo. There was a character in it that looked like me." She shook her head. "Exactly like me."

"And this character, is she still in the game?"

"Sounds like it. That's what Elena called about."

He shook his head. "I knew something was funny about that guy. You've got to call your attorney to start a cease-and-desist action right away." He paused. "Is it a popular game?"

"At the top of the list."

"I'd better called Josh about this. That game and the media surrounding it might bring out more crazies lurking around your place. At least you're not there right now." He slid his arms around her again. "You don't have to fight this battle alone anymore. You have your attorney and you have me. And Josh, and the rest of my team, whenever you need them."

Penelope hugged him. "You have no idea how much this means to me."

"This is what I do, babe. And I do know how much it means to you." He slid a finger under her chin. "Personal safety is a psychological need that people have. It's important for normal people, as well as those who have achieved a degree of notoriety for their work."

"I never went into modeling with the desire to become famous. I only wanted to do a great job, travel the world, and have fun."

Stefan waggled his eyebrows. "Aren't you having fun yet?"

"Not when lunatics are taking shots at me."

"Then we'll have to fix that, won't we?" He nuzzled her neck. "I need to find a way to properly thank you for saving my life, don't I?"

"Depends on what you have in mind. Don't forget the doctor's orders."

"That doctor never had you around to distract him. Help me build a fire and we can lounge in front of it."

Penelope brightened at that idea. "We could play Scrabble again. Your choice, English or Danish."

"If I get a choice, I was thinking more like with or without clothing. The doctor never said we couldn't do that."

Stefan ran his hands down the length of her sides and she shivered with delight just thinking about what fun they'd have when he was feeling better.

21

STEFAN STROLLED THROUGH the charming, cobble-stoned village of Mammoth Lakes near the gondola that led to the top of the ski mountain. He had his arm around the woman he loved and he'd survived a blizzard. How lucky could a guy get? The only thing missing was a resolution to the threat that Penelope faced, but he was making progress on that.

The doctor who was treating him told him that he needed a couple of more days of limited activity, and then he'd be cleared for action again. He'd been able to do a lot from the cabin, working through Josh and the private cyber investigator he'd hired in New York to follow the digital trail. Every day they were getting closer.

This was his first day out of the cabin, and he breathed in the crisp air, enjoying it all. He hugged Penelope close to him, inhaling the fresh smell of her hair and skin. Even without makeup, Penelope was a beautiful woman. Today, she looked so natural, with sparkling tawny eyes, cheeks flushed from the cold, and rosy lips that gleamed with a swipe of lip gloss.

The effect she had on him simply wasn't fair. All she had to do was roll out of bed, and he would fall at her feet. But he loved seeing her dressed up as well. Glancing down at her jeans and tattered parka, he said, "We've got to get some new winter gear for you."

Penelope ran her hands over the brown parka and baggy jeans. "What's wrong with this?"

"Aside from those being ancient jeans and my mother's grungy gardening jacket from twenty years ago, nothing. You can use that to go fishing in with me later on." He stopped in front of a boutique that had skiing outfits and winter fashions in the windows. "Come on, let's go in."

They stepped inside, and Stefan set to work on choosing new outfits for her. "Just think of me as your new stylist," he said, handing a load of clothing to a sales associate to put in a dressing room for Penelope. "Come on, indulge me. It's not like I can go tearing down the mountain with you, though I'd like to. Might as well get your gear ready for the next time we come to Mammoth."

Penelope sorted through what he had chosen for her. "A lot of these ski outfits are more runway than survival-gear style, and isn't that what I really need with you?"

"Oh, I'm not done with you," he said, dragging his lips across her neck. He hadn't even started. Though his physician had outlawed any vigorous activity—including sex—that didn't mean he and Penelope hadn't had their share of romance the past few days. "Just wait until I take you to Cabela's."

"I've done my share of damage there, too," she said, choosing a Bogner jacket to try on.

197

The insulated red jacket with a fur-lined hood had curvy stitched designs on it, along with delicately embroidered yellow and lavender flowers.

"Wow, you've got to take that one," he said. She looked amazing in anything she put on, but she was a professional. "It looks hot with your purple hair."

"It might not stay like this for long, though it has been one of my favorite fun colors."

Penelope ran her hands along the jacket sleeves. "It's beautifully made, and I love it." She picked up an ebony and taupe puffy jacket that also looked good on her, and then she chose insulated pants to match.

While she was changing, Stefan checked his messages, stymied with the slowing progress of Penelope's case. Frowning, he put his phone away, instead turning his attention to selecting sweaters, gloves, and boots for Penelope, along with a few pairs of lined pants and thermal jackets that she could wear any time. She emerged in a new lavender sweater with a dark purple jacket and insulated stretch pants tucked into boots.

"Wow," he said, his spirits lifted. He nodded to the salesperson. "Add that, too."

After depositing their packages in the SUV, Stefan suggested they take the gondola up the mountain and have lunch at the restaurant near the top where the view was astounding.

Inside the gondola, it was warm and packed with happy skiers and snowboarders chattering about their exciting morning ski runs. After they stepped out of the gondola, Stefan paused on the platform side of the restaurant.

He breathed deeply, filling his lungs with crisp mountain air. "This is the life, Penelope. We've got a lot of catching up to do." He hugged her close and then they went inside the restaurant.

The restaurant had floor-to-ceiling glass that looked out over the entire glittering, white-capped mountain range. Skiers glided past on groomed slopes, while snowboarders tackled a challenging course mid-mountain. It was a winter wonderland at play, and he loved it. It was going to be a great season, and he couldn't wait to get up on skis again—next time, with Penelope at his side. He loved her athleticism, fearlessness, and quick wit. He'd never met another woman like her.

Gazing out, he thought of what it would take to safeguard her if the shooter weren't found, or the digital tracking dried up. That wasn't an option, he told himself, determined to do what it took to solve the case and give Penelope her freedom again.

He opened the menu and perused the selections before setting it aside. A waiter stopped by their table. Stefan leaned forward and said, "Would you tell Eduardo that Stefan's here."

"Who's Eduardo?" Penelope asked.

"A friend of mine I ski with sometimes. He's a great chef, too, and always make something special for me."

They chatted, and a few minutes later, Eduardo emerged wearing a white chef's jacket.

"Stefan, heard you had some trouble on the mountain last week. Looks like your head met something harder than it is." Eduardo grinned and held out his hand to Penelope. "Is this the angel who rescued you?"

"Sure is. I'd like you to meet Penelope." If Eduardo recognized her, he didn't give any indication of it.

Eduardo was a tall, dark-haired, good-looking man who'd been happily married for years. Stefan often envied Eduardo and his handsome family, including a lovely wife who'd won an Olympic silver medal for women's downhill skiing and three teenaged boys who'd learned to ski when they were toddlers. During the week, Stefan sometimes skied with the entire family if he wasn't working.

He dreamed of a life like Eduardo had—with Penelope, he hoped. For the first time in years, he was looking forward to building a life with a woman he loved, and it felt good.

"Any dietary requirements?" Eduardo asked Penelope.

"As long as it's healthy and delicious, I'll eat anything," she replied.

"Penelope travels all over the world. Surprise us," Stefan said, sliding his hand over Penelope's. He felt as though his life was finally correcting itself, like a ship that had veered off course in a terrible hurricane and was now finding its true course again. A little battered, but with a lot of voyages yet to be had.

After Edwardo left, Stefan listened to Penelope as she hashed out new career ideas. She was one of the smartest women he knew—and he knew a lot of brilliant female attorneys who were a heck of a lot smarter than he was. He could listen to her talk forever and hoped he'd be so lucky. After blowing it once with her, he never wanted to take that chance again.

Penelope was talking about a new idea for a television series, one that was radically different from the one she'd previously pitched.

"Just look around us," she said. "Look at the people here from all over the world having a great time. When I travel, one of my favorite things to do is to find little shops where they're still making clothes as they did a hundred years ago in that area. Beautiful handiwork that automated factories simply can't match."

She stopped and pulled a violet-colored scarf from her purse. "Look at this scarf I picked up in a little village in Italy. See how fine the needlework is? It's hard to find this anywhere outside of that region in Italy."

"That's incredibly detailed work," he said, inspecting the scarf. "So what's your idea?"

"I want to be the Anthony Bourdain of fashion travel. What he is to local food, I want to be to local fashion. I want to share the world's most beautiful saris and show women how to wrap them, or wear the most incredible Peruvian sweaters made from the warmest Alpaca wool."

Stefan loved watching Penelope becoming excited. He could feel her passion for her craft. "That sounds like a fascinating idea."

"And I think it will sell. At first, I thought I wanted to be on a closed set for security reasons. But I'm not going to let one crazy guy determine what I do with my life." She sat back, resolute in her idea. "While you've been sleeping, I've been talking to potential backers, and I'm pretty sure I can raise the money to produce this. Aimee Winterhaus has already committed to a feature story in *Fashion News Daily* if I launch this. It has international appeal, so I believe it can play in international markets quite well."

"So what's your specific angle?"

"I'm interested in traditional fashion and how it's worn today, and the iconic women from each country who've worn it the best. Lots of designers borrow ethnic looks for their collections. I want to take the camera out and talk to the people who actually create those looks in each country."

"Sounds like half travel log and half fashion show."

"That's right," Penelope said, her face lighting up. "I want to have casual dinners with local artisans, eating local food in charming places and hear them talking about their craft. I'll take the camera into the workrooms, where highly skilled workers practice."

"You might need a bodyguard in some of those places," he said. "I think I can arrange that part of it."

She dipped her head and smiled. "Many times it will probably be groups of women gathered in someone's home to do piece work. That will be fascinating, too. I think other women will love seeing fashion and how it's created and worn all over the world."

"You could call it Global Get-ups."

She poked him in the ribs, chuckling at his silliness. "Something like that. I have the concept, but I haven't thought of a title yet. And this time, Aimee Winterhaus has recommended someone in development who really understands and appreciates the concept." She leaned back in satisfaction.

He couldn't be more proud of her in this moment. Here was

a woman who'd been knocked down—and hard. Her career decimated, hounded by the media, a deranged fan out for blood. Yet she was forging on, drawing on her creativity to create the life she wanted—and deserved to have. If she chose him to be by her side forever, he'd be the happiest man in the world.

When a waiter brought Eduardo's creative dishes to the table, Penelope's eyes widened at vegetables with couscous, pink salmon cooked on a cedar plank, and raspberry and blueberry sauces. "Smells fabulous," she said, touching the tip of her spoon to the sauces. "Oh, these are spectacular."

The aromas swirling around his nose, he gazed over the savory food at Penelope, his gut tightening with desire. He was very nearly the most satisfied man in the world, too.

She looked so happy and they were having such a wonderful time that he dreaded telling her about what he'd learned from the private cyber investigator he'd hired in New York. The evidence was piling up, and soon he thought it would point in a clear direction.

22

WHEN STEFAN TURNED the SUV onto Penelope's street in the Hollywood Hills, she could already feel photographers lurking around, even though she hadn't seen them yet. She'd developed a sixth sense for paparazzi. Anxious about being targeted again in Los Angeles, her stomach tightened as they pulled into her garage. Just when she'd had the chance to relax in the mountains, the online threats were starting again. When would this ever end?

Penelope waited in the car while Stefan opened the door to the house, checking it before she went in. "All clear."

She tapped her phone in her lap and exclaimed with disgust. "Why do I even go on social media anymore?"

Stefan draped his arm over the car door. "More manipulated images?"

"You have no idea. It's absolutely disgusting. I understand my obituary has already been written at several news outlets. Look, I've been voted 'Most Likely to Die' this year." She turned off her phone in disgust.

"The cyber investigator in New York has some leads for us. Let's go in and I'll tell you about what he's found." He kissed her forehead. "My team is working hard to get your life back to normal for you. And for us."

She stepped inside the house, yearning for a swim in her heated pool, but not sure if she should risk it. She'd felt so free in the mountains and found that coming back here was suddenly oppressive. Sauntering into the kitchen, she brought out two bottles of water from the refrigerator. After handing one to Stefan, she opened hers and drank deeply. "When did you find out this information?"

"Few days ago." Holding her hands, Stefan leaned against the kitchen counter.

"Why haven't you told me about this before?"

"Whoa, I've been kind of busy the last few of days," he said, cracking open the cap on his bottle. "Surviving blizzards and concussions. Trying to make love to the woman I've always loved." His eyes sparkled with desire. "The doc's clearing me in a couple of days."

"Flatterer." Penelope couldn't stand not knowing about things that affected her life—good or bad. Was it her imagination, or was he stalling? "You can tell me now."

He drew his fingers across his chin, rubbing it in thought. "We got a lead through Monica."

Penelope stiffened at the mention of his ex-wife's name. What could she possibly have had to do with the events in New York?

"Have you seen her lately?" As soon as the words were out of her mouth, she bit her lip. She hadn't meant for her tone to sound so sharp, but she'd been unaware that Stefan was still in touch with Monica.

Stefan cocked his head and frowned. "No, but if she has anything to add to this investigation, I will. Your safety is paramount to me."

"Then how is she involved?"

"It was a comment she'd made to someone else. I believe Lele Rose was the one who brought it to your attention."

Penelope's lips parted as she began to recall what Lele had said about Monica at Eva Devereaux's party.

Stefan recounted the story. "Monica told another model she was sorry the shooter had missed you, but that you wouldn't get away the next time. Said you were the reason her career is on the decline."

"Wait a minute," Penelope said, narrowing her eyes. "You weren't there. That was a private conversation I had with Lele. Did you talk to her afterward?"

"No, and you're correct. You fired me." A shadow crossed his face.

"Then how did you know about that conversation?"

"Through the device I'd snapped onto your purse, remember?"

She didn't like what she was hearing. "That device you gave me was supposed to alert you only if I needed help. And I didn't need help. I was having a private conversation. Therefore, you were eavesdropping."

His smile slid from his lips. "Come on, Penelope. You know I use high-tech tools. Isn't your safety worth it?"

She nodded half-heartedly. Just being back in her house was unsettling. It was as if a fog blanketed the sunny day outside, and the rational part of her brain had been left in Mammoth. "Then why do I feel creeped out about this? You admitted to reading my text messages. Have you been listening in on all my conversations, too?"

"Of course not. But if I thought you were in danger I would. Penelope, someone tried to kill you. They're still out there. There might as well be a price on your head in the media."

She threw her hands up in frustration. "Is this what you did to Monica?"

Stefan held up his forefinger. "No, but in retrospect, maybe I should have. She had no qualms about cheating on me."

Penelope let her mouth fall open. "Like you cheated on me?" She winced at her own comment. She'd just buried herself, and she knew it. But she couldn't help it. How would they ever get past this?

"I should have told you about the listening device, and I never should have cheated on you. That was the worst mistake of my life. Hurting you nearly killed me. I'll never know what got into me that night," He dropped to his knees and clasped her hand to his heart. "I'm pleading with you, Penelope. If there is anything I can do to make it up to you, please tell me. I have spent years beating myself up for that."

She gazed down at him, pity in her heart. This was a man whose life she had saved only a few days ago. Yet all at once, the old hurt feelings flooded back. Furthermore, he was withholding information and spying on her.

She turned away from him, unable to forgive him, and uneasy about his actions.

Only after their argument did Penelope realize that Stefan hadn't told her about the news from the investigator. Strolling into the garage, she found him putting equipment into the SUV.

"Going somewhere?"

"Back to my place. Josh is on his way over." He didn't look up as he spoke but went about his business.

"Stefan, you were going to tell me about the news from the investigator."

Placing his hands on his hips, he stared at her with his fierce blue eyes. "Josh can brief you on that."

She touched his hand. "What about us?"

"There is no *us* until you find it in your heart to forgive me. I made a mistake but I can't change the past, Penelope. And I can't spend a lifetime with someone who can't move on. Either you trust me to do right by you, or you don't."

Penelope bit her lip and nodded. She'd brought this on herself. They'd had such a magical trip in Mammoth, but within ten minutes of being back in the Hollywood Hills, the magic had dissipated like perfume from a blast of an angry ill wind.

23

THE NEXT DAY, Josh drove Penelope to Bow-Tie restaurant in Beverly Hills, giving her a full briefing of their cyber security findings along the way, which were pointing to off-shore media sites. She listened quietly, desperately missing Stefan; she had spent a sleepless night replaying their argument. She'd checked her phone several times this morning, hoping he might reach out to her, but his decision appeared final.

It was crucial that she find a way out of this mess and move on with her life. Being proactive, she'd called Aimee Winterhaus and had invited her to lunch to talk about her new ideas.

Josh held the door for her as she stepped from the SUV and looked around the front patio at Bow-Tie. The restaurant was busy, with tables of beautiful people chatting and cutting deals in the California sunshine, where on most days, anything seemed possible.

Aimee was already seated at a table under a turquoise striped umbrella with another woman on the patio. Penelope joined them. "Aimee, I'm glad you could meet me."

"Your project sounds so new and fresh that I took the liberty of inviting Talia here," Aimee said, smoothing her precision-cut black bob that had been her trademark style for years.

Aimee was a legendary editor, and Penelope was thrilled she was taking an interest in her idea. She knew it would take a lot of work to make it happen, but she was willing to put in the effort.

Wary of producers now, Penelope wanted to ask the chic, silver-haired woman a few questions. "Talia, how do you feel about reality shows?"

Talia lifted an eyebrow. "They might sell for a while, but you're much classier than that. I hope that's not what you're considering. If it is…"

"No, not at all." Penelope was immensely relieved.

The three women talked about Penelope's concept for the global show. Penelope explained, "We'll showcase international street style and traditional artisans' high quality work. It will be a unique look at how people are taking indigenous styles and putting new spins on them for today."

Talia nodded, her ivy green eyes intense behind her round black frames. "You plan to visit the local craftspeople?"

"That's an important part of the concept," Penelope said. "I want to highlight the workers, too. Many are incredibly talented."

Talia stroked her chin. "That will personalize the craft. We might be able to get some women's groups involved, maybe try to expand trade opportunities for women in underprivileged countries, too."

Aimee interjected. "I think that would be a natural by-product of the show. I can commit to coverage in *Fashion News Daily*.

This is more than a show for Penelope. This can be a global movement to support artisans, too."

They ordered salads and continued talking about ideas. Penelope grew more excited as she listed to Talia and Aimee discuss how they could support the show. She asked for their advice for ideas on how to package the show, and asked Talia if she would be interested in it.

Talia said, "I like the concept and I'd like to buy it, with you at the helm, of course, but I'm not the sole decision-maker. Can you come in and talk with the rest of my team at the studio?"

"Anytime, Talia." Penelope felt like screaming for joy.

Talia went on. "I'll let you know how to prepare. My team can be a tough sell, so you have to be very clear, concise, and enthusiastic. Knowing who your audience is and what they like is especially important, too. You'll get about ten to fifteen minutes and if you hook them, be prepared to answer questions and stay longer. Just steer clear of any talk about tabloid reality shows, even if they sound more excited about that."

"I appreciate your guidance on this." After the disastrous meeting with Cynthia, Penelope was thrilled and thankful that Talia and Aimee understood her vision.

After they finished lunch, the three women gathered their purses and got up to leave. As they were walking out, Aimee said to Penelope, "Are you going to the big yacht party that Kristo Demopoulos is throwing at Marina del Rey tomorrow night? He just arrived and it's shaping up to be the party of the year. He's celebrating the success of Master's Revenge, his new game." Aimee lowered her voice and leaned toward her. "One of the characters looks a lot like you."

"I'm not planning on going." Penelope had been ignoring Kristo's texts. The last thing she wanted to do was visit him on his yacht again. She'd called Scarlett, who was preparing to serve him with a cease-and-desist letter.

"If you change your mind, you can go with me," Aimee said. "We could get some new shots of you for our parties section. It's about time you got some positive press." She put a reassuring hand on Penelope's shoulder. "The negative press can't last forever. Hang in there. I know it's been tough on you."

Penelope assured her she was holding up. It wouldn't do to wallow in self-pity. She said good-bye and stepped into the waiting SUV with Josh.

As they snaked through heavy traffic, ideas for the show percolated in her mind. She had a lot of work ahead of her, but the more Penelope thought about her idea, the more passionate she became about it because it was a win for all parties involved, from the craftspeople and local residents to the designers and those who would buy and wear the clothes and accessories showcased on the series. She loved the idea of helping people and spreading happiness and appreciation, and she had to do something to occupy her mind, channel her energy, and earn a living.

Reflecting on her relationship with Stefan, she realized that because of her inability to trust him, she'd brought many of her troubles on herself. Only she could turn it around now. Yet parts of the story between Stefan and Monica still nagged her. The only thing she couldn't forecast was, would he cheat again? And was she a fool for even considering giving him a second chance?

That evening, Penelope stretched out as she cut though the water in the pool. Josh had wanted to stay with her by the pool, but she'd sent him inside when his phone rang. She needed to let off steam, and she couldn't relax with a bodyguard hovering over her every move. In the pool, no one could see her tears.

Just when she seemed to have a tenuous grip on life again with Stefan by her side, she'd thrown it all away because she simply couldn't bring herself to trust him. She wanted to, and she believed in the essential goodness of him. Would she ever understand *why* he had cheated on her?

She stroked her way through the warm water, the cool autumn air sharp on her shoulders each time her skin broke the surface. After a while, she was exhausted from the frenetic pace she'd maintained.

Lifting herself from the pool, she padded to the outdoor sauna. A blast of hot air hit her when she opened the door. It seemed hotter than normal, but she attributed it to the cool evening air outside. After just a couple of minutes, she could take the extreme heat no more and got up to leave.

The door was stuck, probably because she hadn't used it in a while. She shoved it, and then again, but it didn't budge. Sweating profusely, she tried to adjust the temperature, but the dial had been broken.

This was no accident. Panic welled in her chest, and she screamed for Josh. The sauna was at the rear of her property, removed from the house. Its thick walls were lined with wood. Inside the house, would Josh hear her at all? Wiping perspiration from her eyes, she realized he'd been right about not wanting to leave her alone.

Perhaps sending Stefan away had sealed her demise. Was this the price she'd pay for failing to forgive the man who loved her? The man she loved. What an idiot she had been.

At least her obituary would be ready.

She called for help over and over again, until her throat was raw. Feeling lightheaded, she leaned against the door and jiggled it one last time. However, this time it opened easily under her hand.

"What the hell?" Penelope stumbled outside, drenched in sweat and gasping in the cool air. She plunged into the pool to cool off; though it was heated, it still offered relief.

At that moment, Josh charged through the door. "What happened? Several camera lens were obscured. I was on the phone with the office. I knew I should have stayed with you. "

"No, I'm the one who sent you away. Don't feel bad. When I tried to get out of the sauna, the door jammed."

"You need medical help?"

"Just check the door, will you? It's never stuck like that before." Penelope stepped from the pool and threw a towel around her. Josh had drawn a flashlight from a loop on his belt and was inspecting the door and doorjamb to the sauna. She watched as he ran his hands along the door and tested it.

"It's in good working condition, but there are fresh scrapes. Appears something was jammed in here. Don't use it again unless someone is around." He handed her a robe. "Let's go in, get you to safety. I'll have a look at the security footage. Shall I call the police?"

"No, I'm tired of answering their questions." They went inside and Penelope sat in the safety of her bedroom, gazing out over the twinkling lights of the city below. As she thought of everything that had occurred, and what Stefan had said, she knew what she had to do. She pulled her phone from the pocket of her terry cloth robe.

"Hello Lele, there's something I'd like to talk to you about."

"Doll, I've been thinking about you. How did your meeting with Cynthia go?"

Penelope grimaced, recalling the disaster. "We weren't on the same page. But I have another idea."

"Are you still up for walking in my charity show? I always make good on my word."

"You can count on me." The thought of working again lifted her spirits.

"So what can I do for you?"

"Lele, I'm wondering if you can arrange a meeting for me." She recalled something that Elena had said.

"Sure, doll. I owe you one."

A minute later, Penelope tapped her phone off, feeling satisfied and empowered. She was going to get to the bottom of at least one mystery once and for all.

Josh emerged from the house. "Can't make a positive identification from the footage. Six feet tall, thin frame. Baggy dark jeans and a hoodie." He opened his hand and in it were several yellow sticky notes. "The perp put these over some cameras, but they couldn't reach them all. Do you have any neighbors with security cameras that I can check with tomorrow?"

"I'll give you their numbers in the morning."

Penelope slid into bed, her mind already working on the meeting Lele was arranging for her. Depending on the outcome, this could determine her future.

24

JOSH TURNED THE SUV into Lele Rose's atelier on Melrose Avenue. Penelope peered from the backseat. The popular boutique was an ivy-covered cottage the designer had bought years ago before the street had become popular with international fashion designers. But Lele Rose's designs remained a favorite among celebrities in Los Angeles, especially with younger ones who flocked to her downtown studio in the arts district.

"Park in the back," Penelope directed.

"Sure you don't want me to come in with you?" Josh asked, lowering his sunglasses.

Penelope expelled a breath to calm the jitters in her stomach. "No, I've got this. Better that I meet with her alone. I'll buzz you if I need you." She checked the device attached to her purse to make sure she had the volume turned off.

Lele had been more than happy to set up the meeting for her. "Hope you get what you're looking for," Lele had told her.

Penelope wasn't sure if she would. This could be a complete disaster, but she wasn't backing out now. She straightened her shoulders and stepped from the car to head toward the rear door.

She knew what she had to do.

Lele's office was in the front of the salon. Through the cracked door, Penelope could hear her talking. She waited quietly outside.

Presently, Lele came out and closed the door. When she saw Penelope, she pressed a finger to her lips. "Go on in," she whispered.

Penelope nodded in appreciation and pressed the door open, pausing at the sight of the woman who'd been the source of so much pain in her life.

Monica was even more emaciated than the last time she'd seen her. She wore a short lime green dress with studded, spiked heels. With dirty hair tucked behind her ears and day-old mascara, she looked more Hollywood Boulevard than Park Avenue.

Startled, Monica rose from her chair, shock on her face.

Penelope locked the door behind her.

"What are you doing here? Where's Lele?"

"Relax," Penelope said. 'I have the check Lele promised you." When Lele had called her, Monica asked to borrow money. Lele relayed her request, and Penelope agreed. It would be money well spent, she hoped. Penelope turned her palms up. "Even though you tried to kill me in the sauna."

Monica's mouth fell open, and she vehemently shook her head and jiggled her leg.

"Thanks for having second thoughts," Penelope added in a wry tone, recalling Monica's nervous tic.

"That was only meant to scare you," she said, her voice subdued.

"The photos hit the internet even faster this time." Photos of her stumbling from the sauna, collapsing on her knees from the extreme heat and dehydration before she pulled herself to the pool. *Supermodel Suicide Attempt*, the headlines screamed.

"I don't know anything about that."

"Whether you do or not—and I think you do—that's not what I'm here to talk about." Penelope perched on the edge of the desk in front of where Monica sat. She recalled her earlier attempt years ago at arming herself with a bottle of premium vodka—what Monica seemed to live on—to chisel the real story of how she'd stolen Stefan from Monica's cold lips. It hadn't been a satisfying experience. Would she talk now?

Monica squirmed. "Whatever happened, it was only because I need the money. Nothing personal."

Penelope peered at her. Monica seemed to be shriveling inside of her skin. No wonder she wasn't getting work. Dark circles under her eyes, lackluster hair, sallow skin, jittery nerves—all pointed to one thing. "I don't know what you're on, but you need help."

"I'm not taking anything," Monica said, feigning innocence.

Penelope waved the check in front of her. "This isn't going for drugs."

"I need that," said Monica, rising from her chair and grabbing at it.

"Not so fast. I need some answers first."

As Penelope watched Monica plop down with insolence, the anger she'd harbored for so many years dissolved into pity. She'd once thought Monica had ruined her life, but now she saw that

Monica had ruined her own life instead.

"Tell me about Stefan."

"I've gone through everything he gave me in the divorce." Monica sniveled. "Wasn't nearly enough. I need more money. Can you tell him that? I know he's working for you. And I know how much you make."

If I can ever work again. Penelope let the comment about finances slide. "Maybe I can, *if* I can get through to him." Penelope leaned in closer to Monica. "He's got a big wall around him, and he's really protective of his emotions. If you can tell me how to get to him, then I can help you a lot more. Not just this measly bit." She waved the check again. "You deserve more from him, Monica."

"I do, don't I?" Monica sucked in a breath in anticipation.

"So how can I get to him? How'd you do it?"

Monica hung her head, peeking up at her through her clumped eyelashes. "You hated me for what I did, but I had to, don't you see?"

"I don't hate you anymore." As Penelope uttered the words, she realized they were finally true. She pitied her. "I forgave you. We were friends long before Stefan came around."

"We were, right?" Monica's face brightened. "Well, go ahead, girlfriend. It's your turn at him. And you can take care of me now."

Penelope gritted her teeth in a smile. Monica's thought process was twisted and disgusting. Had she ever known love in her life?

Monica pitched forward in the chair, her elbows on her

knees. "Here's what you do. First, spike his drink. When he wakes up in the morning, rave about how fabulous the sex was." She slapped her leg. "Guys are so macho, they're thrilled to think they got laid."

Penelope stared at her. "You didn't sleep with Stefan that first night?"

"Hell no, at least, not in the biblical way." She snorted with laughter. "Then, you have to stick with them for a couple of weeks." She rolled her eyes. "Yeah, I know. If they think they have a willing partner, they'll be all over you. Stefan was different though. He ran right back to you."

Penelope's skin crawled. How could she ever have been friends with someone like Monica? She'd been duped, too. How many times had she loaned Monica money, though she never seemed to get it back. Monica would repay her with clothes and trips—at someone else's expense. Monica was a swindler, a hustler, a grifter. Penelope forced a conspiratorial grin. "You've done this before with others?"

"Yeah, duh? Most of them pay you off so fast. Some demand a paternity test, so I just move on. Plenty of other suckers out there."

Listening to her, Penelope felt sick to her stomach.

"Next, hang around a free clinic, talk to girls who're pregnant. Works best if they're in the first few months, so you have to get chatty and ask. Tell them you're playing a joke on someone and offer them a hundred bucks to pee on a pregnancy test strip. Brilliant, right?" She started laughing at her plan.

It was all Penelope could do to keep from curling her lips

back in disgust. What a vile, cruel trick. She felt physically ill, but she had to know more. "You weren't pregnant."

"Course not." She made a face.

Mortified at how Monica had played them, Penelope swallowed the bile that threatened to rise in her throat. How could Monica have even imagined such a horrid act?

"Mr. Honesty wanted to do the right thing," Monica said, putting air quotes around her words. "He's such a straight edge."

"After you married, you faked your miscarriage?"

"What do you think?" Monica sat back, satisfied with herself. "Living on easy street, until he got all moral about representing murderers. Like he thought they were innocent. Pu-leez."

"That was truly an amazing plan," Penelope said. *And sick and twisted.* She pressed a hand against her abdomen. She felt like throwing up.

"So do I get the check now?"

Penelope walked to the window, trying hard to digest what she'd just heard. How much of this did Stefan know about? She swung around to face Monica once again. "Did you ever tell Stefan any of this?"

"Do I look that stupid?"

Penelope could hardly speak, and certainly couldn't answer that question. Clearing her throat, she held out the check. "Guess you've earned it."

Monica stood on shaky legs. "If you snag Stefan, maybe Kristo will back off. He's so intense." Monica shivered and reached for the check.

"What do you know about that?" Penelope snatched the

check back.

"If he wasn't so obsessed with you, I'd love to take advantage of him, too."

"Obsessed? Are you talking about the game?"

Monica wiggled her leg impatiently. "He told me you didn't know anything about it."

"What are you talking about?"

"The sauna. All his crazy stuff. New York."

"He put you up to that sauna trick?" When Monica nodded, Penelope stuffed the check in her pocket and grabbed her by the shoulders. "What do you know about New York?"

"I didn't do anything there," Monica cried.

"Was Kristo behind it?"

Suddenly, Monica looked scared. "I-I don't know. Only thing I know is that he always wants pictures. Lots of them. That's all I know."

Penelope couldn't stand to listen to her anymore. She had what she came for, and now, maybe even more. What was Kristo up to? "Here," Penelope said, thrusting the check toward Monica.

Studying it, Monica frowned. "Hey, this isn't made out to me. And where's the rest of the money?" she asked angrily. "What's this address?"

"The rest of the money has been paid to that rehab facility in your name. When you check in, you'll get the benefit of it. And I know someone who has agreed to be your sponsor." Penelope jerked a thumb over her shoulder. "She's waiting, too."

Her anger turning to anguish, Monica whispered, "I don't

need your help."

"Look at yourself, Monica." Penelope replied, wrapping her arms around her old friend. "Look at what you've gotten yourself into."

"It's too late for me. I'm ruined."

"It's never too late." Even for one as psychologically demented and drug addicted as Monica. Given her dysfunctional family background, she'd hardly had a chance. There were programs and medications Monica could take advantage of to lead a healthier life if she wished.

Penelope turned and walked out, holding the door for the sponsor who'd agreed to meet Monica. Glancing over her shoulder as the older woman greeted Monica, Penelope hoped her old friend would get her life together. At least she'd given her a real opportunity.

Josh stood just outside the door. "Everything okay in there?"

"I've got some information for you and Stefan."

"I'll pass it on. The boss is on another job," he added, as he helped her get in the car.

"Where?"

"Not at liberty to say, sorry. But I'll make sure he gets your message." He shut the door and got into the driver's seat.

As Josh backed out, Penelope drew a hand across her forehead. Monica had been almost gleeful in her recounting of the con she'd played on Stefan. The saddest part about it was that Stefan had recognized that Monica needed help and was willing to give it to her, even though she'd taken advantage of him. Did he know the extent of her deception?

When Penelope checked her phone, she saw a message from Talia, asking if she could meet with her team right away.

Frowning, she saw more texts from Kristo. Considering what Monica had said, she leaned forward and touched Josh on the shoulder. "We have a party tonight in the marina."

25

PENELOPE GLANCED AROUND the table at Talia's production team. Here in the office—a converted loft in Los Angeles, everyone was dressed in jeans and t-shirts. Talia had warned her, so she'd worn jeans with heels and a hand-woven sweater she'd found in Ecuador—only one of the countries she wanted to feature on the series.

Talia began. "I invited Penelope here today to tell us about her new project."

Setting aside her nervousness, Penelope began talking about the project she wanted to develop for television. "It's a fashion travel show fusion that focuses on artisan-crafted fashion indigenous to local areas." Once she had their attention, she went on to talk about what a mutual win it would be for everyone involved, from the production team to artisans to viewers.

After delivering her short, twenty-minute pitch, Penelope sat back. "Any questions?"

Several people began talking at once. Penelope answered the questions she could, and Talia addressed others, particularly those that touched on a reality show instead. After an hour, the meeting broke up.

Most of Talia's team raced off to other meetings, but Talia motioned to her to wait while she stepped outside the office to talk to a couple of people in what appeared to be a heated discussion.

Penelope focused on gathering her material and then checked her messages, waiting until they finished. She'd done the best she could, and could only wait for a decision to be made. If Talia's team didn't take it, she had already set up a meeting with another producer she'd once met.

Presently, Talia returned. "Got a few minutes more?"

"Sure." Penelope put down her purse and materials.

"You gave an interesting presentation." Talia inclined her head in thought. "My team raised a lot of good questions."

"You have a smart, thorough team." Penelope had enjoyed answering their questions—and many points they raised had been tough ones.

"I think so, too," Talia said. "Because we've just green-lighted your project. We want to get started as soon as possible."

"That's great. Thank you, Talia." Penelope was so excited to begin working again.

Talia embraced her and said, "Welcome to the team."

Penelope couldn't wait to share her news with Aimee, Elena, and all her friends. Many of them would be at the party tonight.

The sun was setting in the Marina del Rey harbor along the coast of Los Angeles. Streaks of pink, orange, and violet lit the sky, as though in preparation for the party ahead. Penelope sat in the SUV with Aimee next to her, whose camera crew was already on board the glimmering white yacht. Josh turned into the yacht club and showed the guard Aimee's credentials for entrance. The guard waved them through.

Penelope had told Aimee all about her success with Talia's team. "I can't wait to get started," she said, still bursting with excitement.

Aimee listened, nodding in thought. "I'd like to cover some of your journeys, too. Indigenous fashion photo layouts, the stories behind the artisans, aiding women's creative businesses in developing nations. We can coordinate dates with Talia."

"This show has the potential to impact a lot of people in a positive way." Penelope's mind was whirring with possibilities.

Aimee patted Penelope's shoulder. "And viewers will love it. You're naturally engaging."

As they drove closer, Kristo's yacht loomed ahead, radiant in the setting sun.

"There she is," Josh said, nodding ahead toward the sleek yacht moored at the end of the slips. Gargantuan in size, it was too large to fit into a slip. "A Manta Explorer, very nice."

"Two-hundred-thirteen feet," Penelope said. "An amazing vessel." A steady stream of people were flowing down the wooden pier toward it. "Looks like an interesting guest list."

Smoothing her perfect jet black bob, Aimee glanced at the gathering. "That's the Silicon Valley crowd in jeans and t-shirts. No photos there for *Fashion News Daily*—that would be the *No Fashion Daily*." She sighed, and then brightened. "Fortunately, Hollywood stars clean up well. Look, there's Hugo Gutierrez and

Elijah Rousseau with their dates." She began texting her camera crew. "Didn't you say that Elena and Fianna were going to be here, too? I'd like to get them in some shots."

"They said they would be here later."

"There's Monica Graber," Aimee said. "My God, she looks awful."

"She's been through a lot," Penelope said softly.

With Josh trailing behind them, Penelope and Aimee approached the yacht, which was decorated in twinkling party lights and blasting dance music, with giant backlit images of characters in Master's Revenge displayed.

Penelope had formed an agenda, but now she wondered if she'd be able to get Kristo away from the crowd.

As they boarded, Aimee nudged Penelope and nodded toward a giant banner of the warrior character who looked exactly like Penelope. "Better get a shot of that for your attorney."

There was no accident in the likeness of her. With the image enlarged, Penelope could see the same tiny red birthmark under her left lower eyelashes. He'd lifted her image, with complete disregard for her.

As she stared at it, flashes popped in her face.

Aimee grabbed her arm and whirled her around. "I swear those are *not* my people."

"Wait. That's good evidence. Get a photo of this."

Recognizing the opportunity, Aimee had her crew there in a minute to get the shot. "A little to the left, there, that's good. Penelope, the white lace was a good choice. Turn to reveal the open back. There, that's it."

Penelope had chosen a white lace halter dress, onto which she'd affixed a small medallion at the tip of the deep V that was just the right size to insert an audio device.

"What a surprise, Penelope." Kristo's voice sounded behind her. "I didn't know if you were getting my texts. Lose your phone?"

She turned. "It's been a busy week." Kristo was clad in white jeans and a t-shirt, with a black linen sports coat and a crimson silk ascot at his neck.

"Interesting outfit," Aimee said. "I'll need a shot of that."

Kristo held out his arms and spun around. "Like it? I'm dressed as the master from the game." He draped his arm around Penelope and pulled her to him.

It was all she could do to maintain her composure. What she needed tonight was evidence. From the corner of her eye, Penelope could see Josh observing Kristo, sizing him up. She caught herself wishing that Stefan had been here instead.

Kristo gave her a glass of champagne from a tray a waiter brought especially for them. "How're you holding up with all the media attention?" He let his eyes trail over her.

Feeling uncomfortable under his annoying scrutiny, Penelope shifted on her feet. "I don't pay any attention to it." She held the glass to her nose, and then hesitated.

He seemed crestfallen for a second, then regrouped. "But they haven't caught that guy who tried to kill you." He waved his hand around the vessel. "*Mi casa es su casa.* You're welcome to stay here as long as you like."

"Thank you, Kristo, but after this stunt," she glanced up at her giant likeness in a warrior's outfit, "I don't think we play well together."

"I'm the master, Penelope. You might as well accept it. We were meant to be together." He wrapped his hand around her upper arm. "You're not drinking your champagne."

Penelope studied it. "I'm slow." Had he drugged it?

A group of enthusiastic young guys in jeans and t-shirts came up behind Kristo. "Here's the master. Great game, man. Everybody bow down to the master!" As they began mock bowing to him, the movement rippled across the crowd, with people chanting, "Kristo, Kristo."

Penelope let others step between them and slipped away from his adoring crowd. She glanced behind her. Josh was keeping her in his sights.

After draining her champagne over the railing into the water, she hurried through the crowd and made her way to Kristo's office. She tried the door. Locked.

"You never saw me do this." Josh appeared beside her. With a swift movement at the lock, he swung the door open. "Go get what you're looking for. I'll stay here."

Penelope stepped into Kristo's office and headed to his desk, her heart thundering in her ears. The last time she was here, she'd seen a file with her photo clipped to the top. It had struck her as a little old-school for a guy who'd made billions from software.

And yet, there it was again. She ran her hand over it and then flipped open the file, only to find it was empty. As she did, a door to another part of the office slid open. Penelope froze.

No one came out. She walked silently to the dark opening

and entered. Directly in front of her, a light illuminated a floor-to-ceiling image of her in the Master's Revenge warrior outfit. *Creepy.* When she turned to one side, the first image dimmed and another wall lit, casting shadows over a collage of magazine covers.

Turning away, the lights dimmed, and then another wall brightened, revealing a collection of candid shots of her. There she was standing at the podium that night in New York. The fashion show she'd walked in earlier that day. Of her deplaning in Copenhagen, at Tivoli with Elena. There was another image of her going into her family's apartment. Her house in Hollywood Hills, of her swimming in the pool. Having lunch with Aimee and Talia.

How had he gotten these? She swung around, suddenly feeling trapped. Sensors seemed to follow her eyes. Wherever she looked became illuminated. This time the focus was on sensational media headlines, the ones that had been circulating in the media lately.

Spooked by this obsessive display, Penelope backed from the room, and then turned to run.

Kristo caught her by the shoulders. "Don't you like my homage to you? I thought you were worthy of front page coverage. So I arranged opportunities for you."

"You're behind all this," she said, trying to maintain her calm. Kristo was sick. Psychopathic. Her fingers found the medallion she wore. She pressed it.

"It's tiring being second, when you can so easily buy a company and create the news. Instant scoops. Why didn't anyone ever think of that before? Turns out there's a huge amount of money in media clicks, too. As long you have the right headline and cover model."

Penelope jerked away from his grip and threw a glance toward the door, which had been left ajar. *Where was Josh?*

Kristo slowly clapped. "Tell me, when did you catch on to our little game?" He saw her look toward the door. "Oh, your boyfriend had to go."

She'd seen enough. Penelope sprinted toward the open door.

With a swift wave of Kristo's hand, the door slammed shut. He held up his hand. "Clever, huh?" He walked to his desk, to the folder that had her name on it. Open, close. The door to the other room slid closed, then opened again in response. "It's like magic, isn't it? With my renovations, this whole place is like a video game."

Feeling like she'd stumbled into a chamber of horrors, Penelope swung around.

Kristo laughed. "I gave you the chance to come to me in Copenhagen. But you wanted to play hard to get."

"You can still let me walk out of here, Kristo."

Shaking his head, his eyes glittered with excitement. "We can sail the seas together, and you'll never have to deal with another paparazzi again. Or a tedious ex-wife."

"No, Kristo."

"You'll live in luxury with me, your every desire met."

"You actually think I'd leave everything and go down the rabbit hole with you?"

"Why yes." He smiled. "Your apartment is so much nicer

than you imagine, Penelope. It's hardly a rabbit hole. It's a palatial suite worthy of a warrior princess. Worthy of you." He held his hand out to her. "Come, I'll show you. You can get comfortable. You won't be going home anyway."

Penelope inched along the desk, sizing him up. He seemed so calm and confident.

"Open the door, Kristo. I'm not staying here."

Kristo chuckled. "Of course you are. I'm the master of the universe and you're my warrior princess. You are my ultimate revenge on all the women who laughed at me—until I became rich."

"I never laughed at you."

"That's why I knew we'd be perfect together. And this is our world, our command station."

"I'm warning you, Kristo. I don't want to hurt you."

Rotating his shoulder, his eyes gleamed. "Go ahead. I've been in training for this moment." He pushed her shoulders, taunting her.

Penelope jerked aside and shoved her palm up against his nasal septum, spurting blood and snapping his neck back in cervical shock. Following through with her palm, she prevailed, causing him to lose his balance and tumble in a flailing heap.

In a flash, she drew her hand from her cross body purse and pepper-sprayed him in the eyes, leaving him howling. She snatched a couple of power cords from the computer to tie his hands behind his back and secured his ankles.

She knelt beside him. "Let me make myself clear again. I am not staying here. And you will never do this to another woman."

With his eyes reddened and tightly scrunched against the pain, Kristo whimpered. "You can't leave me like this."

She leaned close enough to smell the fear that cloaked him. "Tell me how to open that door so I can get something to wash the pepper from your eyes."

Once he stopped screaming long enough to tell her, she found the manual-open lever and unlocked the door. She tore through the passageway, searching for Josh. She raced up a ladder to an upper deck and stopped.

Rushing toward her was Stefan, followed by several members of the Coast Guard. She raced to him, and he caught her in his arms. Relief flooded her; his arms around her had never felt so good.

"Are you okay?" he asked, alarmed. "We got some intel on Kristo. He's been behind your troubles all along."

"I'm okay, but Kristo needs help." She couldn't help the note of pride that seeped into her voice. "He got some pepper in his eyes."

Watching the Coast Guard arrest Kristo, Penelope finally felt a sense of closure and release. How one person could use sophisticated technology to target her and plant tabloid stories for fun and profit was more than she could have imagined. Kristo might have been brilliant in software, but for whatever reason, he'd crossed over to the dark side.

She glanced up at the enormous lit image of herself in Kristo's warrior game gear and shuddered, realizing how close she'd come to being his captive.

JAN MORAN

Medics were tending to Josh, who'd been knocked out, as well as one of Kristo's accomplice, who was the reason Josh had disappeared from the passageway. Of the two, Josh had definitely fared better. Another officer was questioning Monica, who appeared quiet and withdrawn.

Aimee stood next to Penelope. "It's not often a fashion editor gets a scoop on the most explosive story in business news. *Billionaire Goes Bust,*" Aimee said, sweeping her hands in the air. "Never thought I'd see a billionaire software designer arrested at his own flashy launch party."

"How about *Warrior Princess Exacts Revenge.*" Penelope folded her arms and watched while Stefan spoke to Coast Guard officers.

Stefan was outlining the evidence his cyber investigator had unearthed on how Kristo had created false stories, framing her and other celebrities to game the system and gain exclusives for his tabloid media company's news. They even had the name of the shooter in New York, who was also hired by Kristo, confirming part of Monica's confession.

Add in attempted kidnapping, and Penelope figured Kristo was going away for a long, long time.

"This could be big," Aimee said. "You're a real-life Wonder Woman."

Penelope cast a warning glance at her. "Don't you dare go there. I've already lost one career—my runway work."

"Things sound promising with Talia, though."

"I'm really excited to have to work again, but I have a lot to learn." This was a new world Penelope was stepping into, yet she brought years of experience and street smarts to her role.

Aimee stepped aside, making way for guests who were streaming from the yacht. "Guess nothing breaks up a party faster than when the host is arrested."

"Good thing you had your crew getting photos early."

"Any later and guests start looking sloshed." Aimee peered at two women hurrying toward them. "Look who's arriving fashionably late."

Dressed in Fianna's latest cruise collection of dresses in turquoise and coral, Elena and Fianna were coming aboard, looking shocked. They rushed to Penelope and Aimee.

"As we were walking up, we heard what happened," Fianna exclaimed. "Are you hurt?"

"I'm okay, but Kristo won't be throwing other parties any time soon." Penelope hugged her friends. "He had an apartment on board he was planning to keep me in. That definitely wasn't happening."

"How did you get away?" Fianna asked.

Penelope grinned. "My Krav Maga workouts really paid off."

"Isn't that the Israeli workout you've been trying to get me to do with you?" Fianna asked.

"You have to come with me now." Penelope couldn't stand to think what might have happened if she hadn't had been trained. "What's creepy is that even people you think you know can turn out to be severely mentally disturbed."

"The real pros know how to hide it," Aimee interjected.

Elena seemed particularly distressed. "We were both with

him before—right here on board. He could have kidnapped us then." She clamped a hand over her mouth. "Remember that he was remodeling on a lower deck? Maybe he was preparing for…"

Penelope wrapped her arms around Elena to comfort her. "We're okay, that's the only thing that matters. But I'm taking all my friends to self-defense training."

"Count me in," Fianna said. "I'll get Verena, Scarlett, and Dahlia to go, too."

Aimee touched Fianna's shoulder. "Before we have to leave the premises, I want to get some shots of you and Elena. But we'll have to hurry."

Penelope waited by a railing, mesmerized by the waves far below. She'd never been so frightened in her life, and yet, due to her physical training, she'd known just what to do. If only life and relationships were that simple. How could she protect her heart?

She gazed toward the horizon. If knowing yourself was the most important work you could do in your life, having the ability to read others was a close second. Kristo's intensity, obsessiveness, and grandiosity had been unnerving. These were red flags she'd be wary of in the future.

As for Monica, she was a pathological liar who had no regard for others unless it could benefit her. She was selfish and lazy, but how much of that could be attributed to substance abuse? No telling how long she'd been taking drugs. When they were friends, Penelope had sometimes suspected it, but Monica had always adamantly denied it because Penelope was so against drug use. All she wanted for Monica was to get the help she needed in rehab. Maybe then, the true Monica might emerge, though Penelope would always be wary of her.

The sea breeze kicked up, and she ran a hand over her hair, twisting it at the nape of her neck. The cool air felt good after the claustrophobic rooms she'd emerged from below.

She glanced back at Josh. The medics were putting one of his arms into a sling. She figured she'd stay around to drive him wherever he needed to go.

"You look like you could use some company."

Penelope turned to see Stefan leaning against the rail beside her. Her heart thudded, and without hesitation, she flung her arms around his neck. "What an idiot I've been." He might push her away, and it would serve her right, but she wasn't holding back anymore.

The only way to heal her broken heart was to give it away again.

In response, he clasped her close to him. "You couldn't have known what Kristo was planning," he said. "I only wish I'd been here with you. I never should have left your side."

"That's not what I'm talking about."

Penelope pulled back to face him, wondering how to begin. She would never keep anything from him again. "I had a talk with Monica."

Stefan grimaced. "Do we have to talk about her? It's over. The divorce is final and she's out of my life forever." He kissed her forehead. "I'd rather talk about us, if you'll let there be an 'us' again."

Penelope tilted her face to him, looking him squarely in the eyes. "First, you should know that you never cheated on me. Now I understand why you were so distraught when you came to tell me that you'd slept with Monica. That behavior was completely out of character for you. Because it *never* happened."

Stefan opened his mouth, confusion etched on his face. "But she had the proof. She got pregnant."

"Supposedly."

His brilliant blue eyes clouded with suspicion. "What are you saying?"

"She conned you. Used a date rape drug on you."

Stefan stepped away and ran his hands through hair, clearly distraught. "Are you sure about this?"

Penelope took his hands and nodded. "She confessed to me. Turns out she was never pregnant, either. Monica is a con artist, and she conned both of us."

"That explains a lot," he said, shaking his head slowly. He raised her hands and kissed her fingertips. "Thank you for that."

As his eyes shimmered with love for her, warmth spread throughout her body. "So I thought, how can I not forgive you for something you never did?"

A smile grew on Stefan's lips and he swept his arms around her. "Does this mean we can take up where we left off?"

"I'm planning on it," Penelope said, her heart beating wildly as she touched her lips to his.

- The End -

Style

Sparkle

Read on for a sneak peek at the first chapter of *Sparkle*,
Book #6 in the Love, California series.

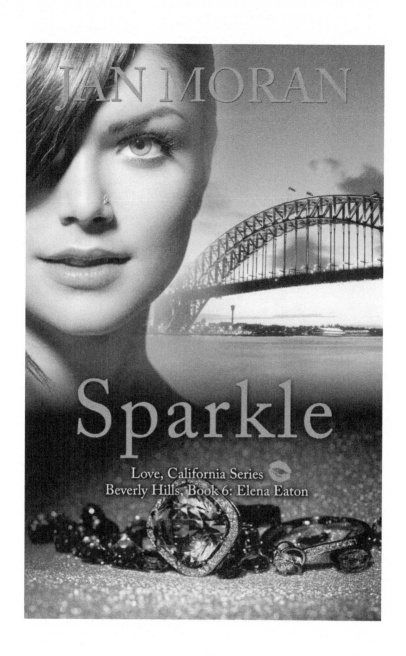

JAN MORAN

Sparkle

Love, California Series
Beverly Hills, Book 6: Elena Eaton

1

Beverly Hills, California

"MORE CHAMPAGNE, MISS?"

Elena Eaton accepted a glass of sparkling bubbly from a server. Veuve Clicquot, she noted, wanting to remember everything about this night. For a girl who'd grown up surfing the waves of Bondi Beach in Sydney, Australia, she never thought she'd be standing in the middle of the brightest stars in Hollywood, mingling and eating caviar at an Academy Awards after-party as if it were what she did every day of her life.

Among the crowd of actors, directors, and producers, little gold statuettes glittered—and yes, they really were much heavier than they looked, she noted—cradled in the arms of the lucky winners who could now command much more per film as an Oscar winner. Most winners had passed the statuettes off to trusted assistants, while a few refused to be parted from their new acquisition.

"Are you enjoying yourself?" asked Aimee Winterhaus, the

editor of *Fashion News Daily* in New York and the host and underwriter of the party.

"I'm thrilled to be here, Aimee."

When the industry insider had asked their friend Penelope where the hottest new place in Los Angeles was to host a private after-party, she had told Aimee about Bow-Tie, owned by her friends Lance Martel and Johnny Silva. The restaurant was in one of a handful of old houses that had been converted to business use on the busy shopping street.

Aimee had hired an event company, and now the entire place looked like a 1920s speakeasy with casino tables, velvet drapes, and glamorous images of Golden Age stars projected on the walls. Not to mention the life-sized ice sculpture of the Oscar statuette. Some A-list actors were gathered at the bar, but many were in a private VIP dining room across from what Elena guessed had once been a large living room. She loved the hardwood floors and the brick fireplaces that anchored the rooms.

"I can't stop looking at everyone," Elena said. "The gowns, the jewelry—"

"The hot actors," Aimee added with a sly smile.

Elena grinned. "Very hot actors." Aimee was right. Her friends in Sydney were going nuts over this. Allison, her best from school, had even organized a viewing party at the bed-and-breakfast she owned with her husband Zach.

"You could meet someone tonight," Aimee said, raising a perfectly arched eyebrow. "The night's young."

"I'm hardly their type," Elena said, twisting her glossy, nude-colored lips to one side. She'd shimmied into a sleek black halter dress that skimmed her hips and fell to the floor, though she felt more comfortable in yoga pants sitting crossed-legged with her sketch pad. Or concentrating at her work bench surrounded by jewelry-making tools. "I'm only glam on the outside tonight."

"Glam is as glam does," Aimee said, laughing. "Trust me, with the right makeup and clothes, we make fourteen-year-old models look like movie stars."

Penelope and Fianna had tried to talk her into a sizzling red dress, but she was so nervous tonight that the last thing she wanted was to stand out in the crowd. Besides, the black velvet showcased the delicate blue diamond necklace and earrings she'd just designed to match her deep blue eyes. And it was slimming, of course. Although she was comfortable in her skin, next to uber-fit celebrities she needed any help she could get.

She touched the stone in her necklace for luck.

Most everyone in the industry tonight had turned out to laud their fellow casts and crews and the night was just beginning. Most people would glide from one party to another—to the *Vanity Fair* party, the Governors Ball, and parties hosted by Lionsgate, Women in Film, and other producers and organizations.

Every event was over-the-top designed; she'd never been to parties like these. Her social life usually involved campfires on the beach, or binge-watching a new TV series with friends. Elena was so excited to be trailing her friend Penelope—a top fashion model—wherever she went.

Equally impressive were the jewels that sparkled on svelte throats, dainty earlobes, and slender wrists and fingers of well-known actresses. Some even wore hundreds of thousands of dollars of gemstones in their hair.

Everywhere Elena looked were shimmering diamonds, emeralds, rubies, and sapphires. Even deep purplish-blue tourmalines. Estimating values, she figured many stars wore jewelry valued at millions of dollars.

So did Penelope.

Elena pressed her hand against her fluttering heart to calm her anxiety. She had pledged her entire business against the jewelry she'd designed for Penelope to wear tonight. Which was why she'd hardly let her friend out of her sight all evening.

She caught Penelope's glance and wiggled her fingers in a tiny wave. Penelope lit up and made her way across the room. Watching her, Elena admired how Penelope moved and showcased her jewelry and dress to perfection. She watched heads turn in Penelope's wake, and heard murmurs of approval trailing her as she passed.

Penelope looked like a glittery mermaid princess who'd just emerged from the sea. She'd even changed her hair color from purple to blond with turquoise and azure highlights to go with the stunning aqua silk gown she wore designed by another friend of theirs, Fianna Fitzgerald.

The blazing marine blue and twinkling green diamonds at Penelope's throat were worth a fortune and had drained Elena of her personal gemstone coffers—not to mention additional stones and the cost of other materials and her labor.

Inspired by opulent jewelry from India, she'd spent months designing the suite that included earrings, bracelets, and rings, but the piece she was most proud of was the lacy, cascading choker with diamonds arranged in a wave-like pattern from light to dark.

Most important to her was the lineage of these fancy-colored diamonds, and what they represented to her family. She'd never shared the true provenance of these stones with anyone outside her family, not even her closest friends. Nor *could* she. In her heart, they would always be Sabeena's diamonds. And in her ancestor's honor, she had marked a large part of their profit on sale for a special cause.

"Elena." Penelope gripped Elena's hands and said hello to Aimee. "Your jewelry and Fianna's dress outshine me tonight," she said, laughing. "They're the real stars."

"You're not a top model for nothing," Aimee said, reaching out to touch the lacy bejeweled choker that Elena had designed. "Those are exquisite fancy-colored diamonds."

"Thanks for wearing them, Penelope," Elena said, in awe of how beautiful Penelope looked tonight. She knew her as a friend, just a regular person she traveled with—most recently when Penelope had come under threat from a deranged psychotic fan by the name of Kristo.

"It's the least I can do," Penelope said, her tawny eyes brimming with elation. "You helped me get through a tough time."

"It turned out well though," Elena said. "How's the new show going?"

Penelope's face shone with excitement. "We started filming, and I'm working on ideas for more episodes. The next one will be Denmark. Isn't that exciting? I'll get to see my parents then."

"Hey hottie, how about more bubbly?"

A familiar voice rang out beside Elena. She turned, widening her eyes in surprise at the sight of an old boyfriend from Sydney, the older brother of her friend Allison. "Shane? What are you doing here?"

"Following the waves." He handed Aimee a fresh glass. "Making my way toward Maui and picking up work along the way." He tapped Elena's nose. "That's new," he said, indicating the tiny, blue diamond nose-stud glinting on her left nostril.

She ignored his comment; he'd lost his right to comment on her years ago. "You're not working at Bow-Tie regularly are you?" This was her favorite restaurant, and she'd die if she had to see him here all the time.

"Just the big party," he replied with a wink at her. Turning to Penelope, he said, "That's quite the jewelry you're wearing. Big rocks, there." He let his eyes slide over Penelope.

"Keep your eyes and your hands to yourself." Elena wanted to slap the floppy blond hair right out of his eyes. Tan and buff, he was a surfer dude out for fun. And faithful to no woman. His sister couldn't be more different.

Penelope laughed off his remark with grace. "You're a friend of Elena's? These are her designs."

"Not a friend," Elena said, scolding him with narrowed eyes.

Ignoring her expression, Shane gave her a smooth grin. "Nice work, Elena. Taking a step up in the world, are you?"

"Don't you have work to do?" The last thing she needed tonight was Shane hovering around. She was on edge enough as it was. As cute as he was, no way would she fall for his tricks again.

Shane wagged his brows and sailed through the crowd, stopping to flirt with every attractive woman.

"Good riddance," Elena muttered.

Aimee looked at her with amusement. "Don't let him get to you."

"I won't," Elena said, flipping her hair from her forehead. She had more to worry about than Shane.

"As for the new nose bling, I love it," Penelope said.

Aimee nodded. "Very sexy. Accents your eyes."

"I've got to run, too," Penelope said. "My producer wants me to meet some people." She smiled. "But I'm posing for every picture I can for you and Fianna."

"Lovely to see you shining so brightly after that awful mess, Penelope." Aimee leaned in to air kiss the model goodbye.

Nervous didn't even begin to describe how Elena felt. Terrified was more like it. Yet the exposure from tonight and an important jewelry sale could elevate her struggling business into the stratosphere, secure her family, and more. She hoped an offer for her work would come in after photos circulated.

"Just look at that Chanel. Simply sublime." Aimee waved and nodded at several attendees she knew. "Besides the Met Gala in New York and the Cannes Film Festival, this is the best place to photograph stars in the most beautiful attire."

"And jewelry," Elena said, glancing around in appreciation.

Aimee ticked off her fingers. "The European designers are out in force. I've seen Chanel, Dior, Armani Privé, Valentino, Louis Vuitton, Gucci, and Givenchy. And the Americans are here with Carolina Herrera, Monique Lhuillier, Ralph Lauren, and

Lele Rose."

Taking a breath, Elena asked, "Which outfit do you like best?"

"I'd have to say Penelope's. Fianna has a fresh, new point of view."

Elena gazed at the fluid, aqua silk dress Penelope wore that Fianna had fit to her. She also admired how Penelope wore the diamond set—or *parure*—she'd designed.

In rare fancy colors ranging from deep vivid blue to greyish blue, from sea foam green to forest shades—colors rivaling the legendry Hope and Dresden Green diamonds—the stones were set in platinum that glittered against Penelope's glowing skin. The delicate choker rose high on her neck and draped across her collarbone, dipping to her décolletage.

This was her masterpiece, simply the finest work she'd ever done.

Her heart quickened at the brilliance of the natural stones, faceted to perfection, framing Penelope's long, graceful neck. Jewelry design was Elena's artistic expression. She loved the luminosity of gemstones, the precision work of design, and the sheer beauty of creation.

The patina of history swirled about the world's most famous gemstones, adding luster to remarkable stones. From the whispered curses of the magnificent Koh-i-Noor and Black Orlov diamonds, to the incredible Star of India—a star sapphire the size of a golf ball—to the heart-shaped Taj Mahal Diamond that Richard Burton had bought for Elizabeth Taylor. As well the La Peregrina Pearl that Taylor's beloved dog almost swallowed.

Elena loved all the stories.

Her gemstones had their own secret history, too. And now was their time.

For months, she and Fianna had worked together to create the most visually stunning, coordinated ensemble on the red carpet for Penelope. They had neighboring shops on Robertson Boulevard and often worked long into the night together. If Penelope's photographs were chosen as fashion magazine leads, their countless hours of hard work and huge financial gamble would pay off.

Smiling with satisfaction, Elena saw another person admiring the choker on Penelope. She couldn't have asked for a more perfect model and showcase for taking her jewelry line to the next level, so she'd invested everything she had—and could borrow—into it.

"Penelope looks perfect tonight," Elena said. "Wouldn't she make a great cover?"

"Absolutely." Aimee smoothed her sleek black bob and held a finger to her red lips. "As a matter of fact, Penelope *will* be our cover next week. You should see the red carpet photography we got. And your jewelry is dazzling. Get ready to write orders, darling. Your pieces are bound to get snapped up by some billionaire."

Elena was so excited she bear-hugged Aimee, the imperious industry editor many designers were nearly afraid of. "I'm so excited, thank you!" She fervently hoped her work would be sold. She had been knocking on retailer doors for years with limited success. Either she hadn't had a big enough name, or she couldn't produce the volume they needed.

Elena had been saving her money a long time for this expensive wager. So when Penelope had offered to wear her designs—and Fianna's—both women jumped at the chance.

Elena had known that only diamonds would do. She glanced around. Fianna was somewhere in the crowd, mingling and having a great time.

Aimee moved on to greet another winner just as Elena's phone buzzed in her purse. A text message popped up on her screen from her cousin Coral in San Diego. *OMG! The entire Bay family watched the Academy Awards. Saw Penelope Plessen on the red carpet. Jewels are AMAZING!*

Elena smiled at her cousin's message. Her mother, Honey, had grown up in San Diego. Elena had loads of aunts, uncles, and cousins in the area. *Too many Bays on that shore*, her dad often said. She loved his corny jokes, and that's where she'd gotten her sassy mouth, her mother claimed.

Just then another text appeared from Coral's sister, Poppy, a journalism student who was handling her publicity. *Get photos!*

Elena grinned. She couldn't wait to tell Poppy about Aimee and the *Fashion News Daily* cover.

As she texted her cousins, Elena kept an eye on Penelope. Her boyfriend Stefan, who owned a bodyguard service for the rich and famous, kept close to her. Still, she was anxious every time she thought about the fortune around Penelope's neck. She couldn't help but think what might happen. Every possible disaster had crossed her mind.

"Hey, why the frown?" Fianna appeared next to her, her long

red hair framing her face in loose curls.

"It's just my imagination running bonkers again." Elena gave an unsteady laugh.

Fianna nodded toward Shane. "He's sexy. Saw you talking to him. Someone you know?"

"Someone I never wanted to see again. I dated him in Sydney when we were teenagers." She shuddered. "First kiss." Changing the subject, Elena said, "Penelope is such a professional. Look at how she moves in your dress."

"This is more than I dared to dream about." Fianna let out a little squeak of excitement.

Elena nudged her and winked. "Can you believe this is happening?"

"I need lots of pictures. I might never make it here again." Fianna gripped Elena's hand in excitement. "Can you believe it? I met a costume designer who was gushing over Penelope's dress." Not waiting for an answer, Fianna glanced at her. "Looks like you have a real problem. Your champagne glass is empty and you need dessert. Come with me."

Elena hesitated, not wanting to let Penelope out of her sight. "Bring me something?"

"You can't stare at Penelope all night. We need to meet other celebrities, too. There's a lot of potential business here."

With reluctance, Elena acquiesced. "You're right."

Fianna took her hand and led her toward a table laden with delectable treats that Lance and his kitchen staff had made. Exquisite miniature fruit tarts, tiny crème brûlées, chocolate mousse, gold foiled statuettes. "Yum," Fianna said, picking up a plate.

Glancing back, Elena saw Stefan excuse himself from Penelope, motion toward another one of his bodyguards who was also in attendance for another star, and walk toward them. He looked handsome in an ebony tuxedo that showed off his broad shoulders and trim waist. Elena was happy for Penelope that she'd reconnected with the love of her life.

Stefan slowed by them. "Having fun, ladies?"

"Best time ever," Fianna said.

"I'm still pinching myself," Elena added. "Penelope is a vision."

"Isn't she?" Stefan gazed after her, admiration evident in his eyes.

Elena traded a look with Fianna, and they both released a little sigh. With all the gorgeous women in the room, Stefan's heart was firmly tied to Penelope. And they had nearly missed the chance to reconnect.

She had never dated a man who looked at her the way Stefan looked at Penelope. The surfers she'd dated in Sydney and San Diego only wanted big waves and good times.

Drawing a shaky breath, Elena leaned toward Stefan. "I'm jittery just watching Penelope. My entire net worth and everything I could borrow is hanging on her neck and earlobes."

"Relax, Elena, we've got this." Stefan winked and moved on toward the restrooms.

She certainly hoped so. When she was young, she'd started making jewelry as a sideline to support her surfing habit, but soon became more enamored with designing new pieces than chasing waves. After saving her money, she'd traveled to the San Diego area to study at the Gemological Institute of America—the GIA—in Carlsbad where she honed her skills in gemology and jewelry design. She'd worked hard to become a world-class designer, and now, here she was on the brink of success. She hoped.

"Don't look so stressed," Fianna said. "Think of all the opportunities here."

Elena caught her breath again, hardly believing this night was real. By the time tonight's photos hit social media, newspapers, and magazines, her world could change.

She couldn't let her parents down either. They'd invested their savings in her vision, too. She shouldn't bypass any chance before her. "Guess we better circulate."

"We might as well indulge first," Fianna said, selecting a raspberry tart. "We don't have to worry about being photographed like the stars."

Elena eyed a trio of chocolate delights. "This is why I work out." She chose a miniature dark chocolate sculpture of a movie reel decorated with sea salt and raspberries.

"Hey you two."

Turning around, Elena's frown dissolved into a wide smile at three women who'd just joined them. Exchanging air kisses and hugs, she greeted her friends. That afternoon, Fianna had closed her boutique and they'd all gathered there to get dressed and made up.

Penelope had brought in hair stylists and makeup artists from High Gloss, and Fianna had her alterations staff there to help her clients and friends choose dresses from her racks and make any last minute adjustments. They'd blasted music and everyone had been in such high spirits. Lance and Johnny from Bow-Tie had sent salads and sandwiches, which Elena had been too nervous to eat.

Elena was so glad they were all together sharing this special night. Verena and Scarlett were dating the partners at Bow-Tie, Lance and Johnny, so they'd been able to get in. As for Dahlia, her grandmother Camille knew all the celebrities from years ago to the present. "How'd it go at the High Gloss station?"

"It was so exciting to talk to all the stars," Verena said. She was wearing a royal blue one-shoulder dress that reflected her eyes, and her pale blond hair curved around her face. "Many of them were nervous, so we found ourselves calming them." She turned to Fianna. "And everyone loved our dresses. They all know your name now."

Penelope had suggested to High Gloss Cosmetics CEO Olga Kaminsky that she bring in Verena and Dahlia to provide skincare and perfume to accompany the High Gloss color line at backstage makeup stations at the awards. Artists were providing touchups for the stars before they went on stage. Between tears and perspiration, some of the actors were a mess.

"I got so many selfies," Dahlia said. "Can you believe it— the *stars* were suggesting it." She looked stunning in a strapless, emerald green dress and earrings to match that Elena had custom designed for her a couple of years ago. Dahlia's grandmother Camille had commissioned the earrings as a birthday surprise.

"That's because they found out she's dating Alain Delamare and a lot of them are Formula 1 fans." Scarlett tapped Verena on the shoulder and laughed.

"I hardly said a word," Verena replied. "People recognized Dahlia from that finish line kiss in Monaco that was blasted around the world. They kept saying, 'haven't I seen you somewhere before?'" Her lip curved in a mischievous smile. "I just helped them remember."

As they talked and laughed, Elena continued to glance at Penelope. Guests moved between them as the party went on. She didn't see Stefan, and she began to wonder what was keeping him, though she knew he had other clients there, too, as well as other bodyguards on staff discreetly standing by.

Scarlett noticed her unease. "Relax, Elena."

"There are so many people." Of all her friends, Scarlett, her business attorney, knew exactly what was at stake.

While her friends talked, Elena searched the crowd, watching Penelope again as she moved from one group to another. Her vision was blocked by a tall, thirty-something guy in a tuxedo. With glossy black hair and a trimmed shadow of a beard, he turned and caught her trying to peer past him.

She couldn't be sure, but she thought Penelope might have disappeared into the private VIP room.

"Looking for someone?" His brow furrowed as if she'd interrupted him.

Elena stepped aside and looked past him. "I'm good."

"Maybe. But not what I asked."

"Excuse me?" She'd just dealt with Shane and didn't need another inconsiderate oaf to spoil her evening. Not that neither of them could.

He stepped into her line of sight. "Are you here alone?"

Elena put a hand on her hip. "If that's a pick-up line, you'll have to do better than that, mate." She blinked. *Was that the champagne talking?* He was nice-looking, if you liked that sort of brooding thing. Which she didn't.

His eyes slid down her neck, and the crease between his dark brows deepened. "I'm Jake."

Where *was* Penelope? She'd lost sight of her.

"And you are?"

"Definitely looking for someone else." Elena fidgeted with her necklace, sliding her fingers over it as if to protect it from his view.

"Actress?"

"Excuse me." She stepped to one side, but a passerby bumped her back into the man of a hundred questions and she toppled off her high heels, sloshing champagne on his shirt. "Oh, bugger—"

"Got you." He steadied her.

"Sorry." She dabbed his shirt with her napkin. She couldn't help but notice that he was pretty firm under there. Probably spent his days working out. A bar bouncer, if she had to guess. Or actor, she corrected herself, remembering where she was.

He caught her hand. "It's okay."

He plucked the crumpled napkin from her hand.

"Jason, I'll get another—"

"Jake." Shaking his head, he stepped to a nearby table and grabbed a cloth napkin. "Actresses," he muttered.

"I heard that. What makes you think I'm an actress, and

what's wrong with that?" She knew a lot of working actors—women and men—and they were dedicated to their craft. Some became big stars, but for most of them, it required discipline to maintain a modest living doing what they loved.

Jake swung around. "First, you're pretty in a glossy sort of way, second, you were talking to Penelope Plessen and Aimee Winterhaus—though you're not thin enough to be a model—and third, that's definitely not your own jewelry."

Elena's lips parted in astonishment. *How presumptuous.* "Look, mate, I'll have you know—"

Suddenly, the closed door to the VIP room flung open and screams erupted, piercing the music that throbbed above the incessant chatter. Some of the biggest celebrities flooded from the room, tumbling over each other to get out.

A woman stumbled out in shock. "We've been robbed!"

In the commotion, the woman next to Elena stepped on her hemline. Her heel caught in the fabric and jerked Elena down hard, pinning her to her spot.

"Damn it," Jake exclaimed, just as Elena flailed backward. His strong arms wrapped around her, keeping her upright, but his attention was riveted across the restaurant.

"Where's Penelope?" Every worry she'd had suddenly surged to the surface.

"Stay here," Jake said, yanking her skirt free and leaving her. He cut through the pandemonium toward the VIP room.

"There she is," Fianna said, pointing across the room.

Elena stood on her tip-toes to see past the throngs of people scurrying about. "Oh no…"

Across the room, Penelope had emerged from the VIP room, where other stars were also looking frightened and dazed. Her hands were clasped around her bare throat.

Her necklace was gone.

Elena cried out in anguish and pushed toward Penelope, who sank to her knees on the floor, her head in her hands, now bare of the stunning ring and bracelet that Elena had created. From the corner of her eye, she saw Stefan racing toward her with Jake not far behind.

"Penelope!" Elena cried out, her heart pounding as she watched Penelope go limp in Stefan's arms. She'd only taken her eyes from her for a minute. Oh, why hadn't she insisted on staying with her?

She'd never forgive herself if her friend had been hurt.

To continue reading *Sparkle*, visit your favorite retailer.

About the Author

JAN MORAN IS a writer living in sunny southern California. She writes contemporary and historical fiction. Keep up with her latest blog posts at JanMoran.com.

A few of Jan's favorite things include a fine cup of coffee, dark chocolate, fresh flowers, and music that touches her soul. She loves to travel just about anywhere, though her favorite places for inspiration are those rich with history and mystery and set against snowy mountains, palm-treed beaches, or sparkly city lights. Jan is originally from Austin, Texas, and a trace of a drawl still survives to this day, although she has lived in California for years.

Her books are available as audiobooks, and her historical fiction has been widely translated into German, Italian, Polish, Turkish, Russian, and Lithuanian, among other languages.

Jan has been featured in and written for many prestigious media outlets, including *CNN, Wall Street Journal, Women's*

Wear Daily, Allure, InStyle, O Magazine, Cosmopolitan, Elle, and *Costco Connection,* and has spoken before numerous groups about writing and entrepreneurship, such as San Diego State University, Fashion Group International, The Fragrance Foundation, and The American Society of Perfumers.

She is a graduate of the Harvard Business School, the University of Texas at Austin, and the UCLA Writers Program.

To hear about Jan's new books first and get special offers, join Jan's VIP Readers Club at www.JanMoran.com and get a free download. If you enjoyed this book, please consider leaving a brief review online for your fellow readers.

Made in the USA
Monee, IL
16 January 2022

89097296R00156